DEATH GOES
OVERBOARD

Phillip
Martin

By the Author

Death Comes Darkly

Death Goes Overboard

Visit us at www.boldstrokesbooks.com

DEATH GOES OVERBOARD

For Drew — one of my favorite fans!

David S. Pederson

by

David S. Pederson

LIBERTY
·· EDITION ··

A Division of Bold Strokes Books

2017

DEATH GOES OVERBOARD

ISBN 13: 978-1-62639-907-5

This Trade Paperback Original Is Published By
Bold Strokes Books, Inc.
P.O. Box 249
Valley Falls, NY 12185

First Edition: April 2017

Credits
Editor: Jerry L. Wheeler
Production Design: Stacia Seaman
Cover Design by Sheri (graphicartist2020@hotmail.com)

To my husband, Alan,
and to my wonderful family and friends, I thank you all.
And special thanks to my editor, Jerry Wheeler,
who keeps my i's dotted and my t's crossed.

Chapter One

The MacDonald/Henning case glared up at me from my desk, daring me to file it away for the day. It was only a petty larceny case, but I knew I should do some more research on it in spite of the heat and the fact that my shift was almost over. Mr. MacDonald and Mr. Henning had been bilked out of a fair amount of money, and my job as a Milwaukee police detective was to investigate, though the leads on the perpetrator were few and far between at this point.

A bead of sweat ran down my forehead as I stared at the folder. I picked it up, closed it, and used it to fan myself as I glanced about the detectives' room. Most of the desks were already empty, their occupants either out on cases or finished in the office. The chief had checked out an hour ago. I rocked back in my old wooden chair, listening to it squeak and groan, and watched the ceiling fan above me revolve far too slowly, keeping pace, it seemed, with the large wall clock opposite where I sat. 3:25 p.m.

With one final fan of the folder, I brought my chair back down and filed the case away for another day. "Sorry, Mr. MacDonald and Mr. Henning, but your case will have to wait. It's close enough to quitting time, in my opinion." I straightened up my desk, covered my typewriter, and tore off the calendar page so it would be ready to go for tomorrow. Wednesday, May 28, 1947, went in the trash can next to my chair. I grabbed my fedora and suit coat and went downstairs, where the desk sergeant was typing reports and looking just slightly more miserable than I did.

"Hey, Sol."

"What can I do for you, Detective?" he responded, without glancing up from his typewriter.

"I'm finished for the day. Feinstein's on call. I'll check in for messages later."

Sol looked up at me then. "Lucky you. I still have two hours of reports to type, and then I'm on the desk until eight and my back is already killing me."

"Sorry to hear it."

"You and me both. Move that fan more this way before you go, will ya?" He nodded toward a rusty old electric fan on top of the file cabinets behind his desk.

I walked over and shifted it a little more toward him. "How's that?"

"Eh, no difference, but thanks anyway. Going to the exhibition game tonight out at Borchert Field?"

"Nah, I'm taking my aunt to tea."

The sergeant spun around in his chair and looked at me. "Tea? Well, la-di-da, Detective."

I smiled. "Not my idea of fun, Sol, but it's our once-a-month date. Keeps her happy."

"To each their own, I guess." He spun back around and typed a few more sentences.

"How about you? Going to the game?"

"I don't get off until eight, and it will be half over by then. I'll catch some of it on the radio. Tea, huh?"

I shrugged. "She likes it."

"Dames, gotta keep 'em happy, I guess, though I'm not sure aunts qualify."

"This one's pretty special, Sol."

"She must be. When I get outta here tonight, I'm heading home and popping open a nice cold one. You won't catch me having tea, especially in this heat."

"Have a cold one for me, too."

"I might have two for you. Don't forget to sign the board."

"Right." I picked up the chalk and put my initials in the out box beside my name, Heath Barrington.

"Later, Sol."

"See ya, Detective."

My old Buick Century was parked in the back lot, and I was soon headed east on State Street all the way to Marshall, then south to Wells and my Aunt Verbina's apartment in the Cudahy Tower. I left the car in the shade of a No Parking zone, which is one of the luxuries of being a cop, and went upstairs to escort her down. The two of us were soon headed to the Pfister Hotel six blocks west.

"Don't put your window down, Heath. I just had my hair done. You can leave the vent window open, but that's it."

"Yes, ma'am." I glanced over at her, sitting up straight and proper in the seat beside me, her gloved hands folded atop her pocketbook in her lap. She wore a smart hat with a red plume that just brushed the roof of my car. To complement that, she had put on a dark brown bolero jacket over a white blouse, both of which accented her beige skirt. Her earrings matched her broach which went nicely with her pearls. Aunt Verbina was nothing if not stylish, and I guess I got that from her.

It was just a few minutes before four when we reached the grand old hotel.

"Use the valet parking, Heath. It's impossible to find good parking on the street, and I don't want to walk in this heat."

"Yes, ma'am." I hated spending the money when I could park on the street at a penny meter, but I dutifully did as instructed.

I stopped under the awning and gave the keys to the valet, a young kid not much older than my car, I thought. He took them with a rather disdainful look at my old Buick.

"What year is that, mister?"

"1938, Buick Century, series 60."

"Time for a new one, war's over."

"Tell that to my bankbook, kid."

He handed me a claim ticket, which I slipped into my pants pocket before going around to help Verbina out. She took my arm as we strode up to the lobby door, where a doorman in a cap and coat of navy blue with brass buttons opened it for us, smiling at my aunt.

"Good afternoon, Mrs. Partridge, nice to see you again. A warm one today, isn't it?"

"Yes, it is, thank you. Nice to see you, too," she replied, but from the look on her face I was pretty sure she did not recall seeing him before. I gave him a polite nod as I removed my fedora, declining to check it, and followed her into the beautiful lobby, which was noticeably cooler. The maître d' welcomed us to the dining room with similar formal familiarity and ushered us to a table. My aunt was a regular here, and I looked forward to Wednesday afternoon tea with my Aunt Verbina in spite of what I had told the desk sergeant.

"Tell me, Travis," she said to the maître d', reading his name off his engraved gold badge though he had seated her dozens of times in the past, "is that handsome waiter I like so well still here? You know, the one with the English accent."

"Ah, you mean Seth, Mrs. Partridge. I'm sorry to say Seth has left the Pfister just last week."

She pouted her too-red lips. "Oh, that is too bad. He always took such good care of me."

"I'm sure you will like Gilbert, madam. He will be waiting on you today." Travis handed us petite menus with gold tassels and placed our napkins in our laps, which made me feel rather silly. I put my hat on one of the empty chairs at our table and unbuttoned my suit coat with a happy sigh.

"I will send over some ice water for you tout suite." He smiled graciously and maneuvered through the tables back to his station at the lobby door.

"Oh, it really is a shame, Heath. No one can keep good help anymore."

I nodded. "Since the war ended, there's been no lack of men looking for work, though, so jobs don't go unfilled long."

"Oh, that war—so horrible. The war to end all wars, they say. I certainly hope so. Let's not talk of it today."

A busboy appeared with water and then disappeared just as quickly after filling our glasses.

"Honestly, did you notice a button missing off that busboy's right cuff?" Verbina whispered to me. "What is the world coming to if a place like this can't keep decent help and make sure their employees are groomed and dressed properly? Thank goodness Randy is still here. A good maître d' is so important."

"Travis."

"Yes, yes, Travis. That's what I said, isn't it? Remind me to have a word with him after tea." She rummaged in her pocketbook, but she didn't find what she was looking for, so she set it back upon the table next to her water glass. She picked up her menu and scanned it rather briefly. "Let's see, I think I'll have the Earl Grey and some warm scones with jam. Oh my yes, that does sound delightful." She closed the menu and set it on the white linen tablecloth on the other side of her purse.

"Isn't that what you always have, Auntie?"

"If you find something you like, why keep trying other things?"

"Not to mention you didn't bring your reading glasses, so you can't see the menu."

"Don't be cheeky, Heath. You know perfectly well I don't need glasses. They just make the print on these menus too small. What will you have?"

I grinned at her. "I'll have the same thing you're having."

"Lovely. Oh, and get us some heavy cream. You have to ask for it special now—they used to bring it automatically."

I gestured for Gilbert and gave him the order, then leaned back in my chair with a sigh, looking at her. "Gilbert seems capable."

"Oh, they all seem quite capable at first. It's too soon to tell."

"Still, he seems nice."

Verbina shot me a look. "Rather dashing, too, I must say."

I blushed just a touch. "If you say so. He presents a nice image for the hotel."

Verbina pulled off her white gloves and laid them on top of her pocketbook. "Speaking of image, Heath, I think it's high time you seriously start to think about changing yours."

"My image?"

"Yes, yes. I mean, for goodness sake, you're over thirty and you've never been married or even had a steady girlfriend."

"Oh please, Auntie, not you, too. I get enough of this from Mom and Pop. Besides, I'm hardly an old man."

"No, of course not. You know I don't often agree with

your parents, and I understand about you more than they do, more than even you think I do, if you follow me."

I nodded, but I wasn't entirely sure.

"All I'm saying, Heath, is that a man in his thirties in your position needs to think about settling down and having children. And here you are, barely begun. You're going to have big responsibilities now, and you're starting to get big cases at the station. You won't have time to go flitting about."

"I don't think I've ever flitted about, Auntie."

"Oh, you know what I mean. You'll need to attend certain functions like the policemen's ball, for one. Who will you escort? These are things you need to think about, Heath."

I rolled my eyes. "Oh, Aunt Bina, please. I've never attended the policemen's ball, and I don't intend to start now—not that I have anything against policemen's balls." I waited for her reaction, but it clearly went over her head.

"There are other things to think about besides that. I know several nice young ladies that would be ideal for you."

"Oh, my. You're not going to try and fix me up, are you?"

"Fixing up is exactly what you need, Heath Barrington, though it's beyond me what needs fixing. You're young, tall, handsome, witty, and bright, and you've certainly got the charm. The women should be throwing themselves at you, and they are, but you barely notice."

I fiddled with my napkin. "I've been busy."

"No man is that busy, and you don't have to make excuses. This is me you're talking to, not your parents."

"I know that. And aren't you the one who always told me to be true to myself? To question everything? To not blindly follow the pack? To live my life to the fullest, to be happy with who I am, how I am?"

She rolled her eyes and sighed impatiently. "Of course, darling, of course. But you're in a position now where you're getting noticed, and I think it's important for you to put on a good front, at the very least. Not everyone thinks the way we do, in case you haven't noticed. I'm not trying to change *you*, my dear, just your image."

Gilbert arrived with our tea, scones, assorted jams, and heavy cream, and I was happy for the interruption. He gave me a dazzling smile, not unnoticed by Verbina. As he walked off, I forced my attention away from Gilbert's behind.

"I worry about you, my dear nephew, I truly do."

"What's wrong with being a bachelor?"

"A bachelor in his twenties is fine. A bachelor in his thirties is all right, but a bachelor in his forties…"

"I'm not in my forties yet, Aunt Bina."

"Today, no, but soon. And if you don't take certain actions, you'll quickly be a confirmed bachelor, and people will talk."

"People already talk. Mother calls it my shyness with the ladies, Father calls it peculiar."

"She says tomah-toes, he says tomatoes. They've both asked me to talk to you."

"Why? Because I'm a tomato, a fruit?"

"Tomatoes are vegetables, not fruits."

"They seem like a fruit to me, and like me." I grinned mischievously at her.

Verbina scowled. "Stop being so cheeky, it's annoying. Your parents think you should be married, Heath. Frankly, so do I."

"Why on earth do you think that? You of all people."

"As you just said, people talk." She sipped her tea, watching me over the top of the cup.

"I know that, but so what? Let them talk, what does it matter?" I spread raspberry jam on a warm scone, trying not to let any drop on the crisp white tablecloth or on my new tie.

"It matters because people start to wonder. They gossip,

and it can affect your future. People ask why you never seem to get out with some pretty young thing."

"What people?"

She set her lipstick-marked cup down on the saucer impatiently. "Oh for goodness sake, Heath! People people. All I'm saying is it wouldn't hurt for you to get out more, be seen with some lovely girl on a regular basis. I think you could manage at least an occasional date."

"Well, thank you for that," I said, biting off the end of a scone.

"Oh, don't get defensive. I'm only looking out for your own good. A man who finds himself in your position could go places, do things. You just need a good, strong woman to drive you."

"You're a strong woman, Aunt Bina."

A heavy sigh escaped her red, red lips. "You need a wife, Heath. People expect you to be married. That's all there is to it."

"Why? Why do I need a wife? I live my life discreetly. You're the only one I talk to about these things."

"Pass me the sugar. Discretion is absolute, but you must keep up appearances."

I passed her the sugar bowl. "Is that what this is about, keeping up appearances?"

"My dear, that's what it's always been about, always will be about. People don't marry for love or because someone is attractive or interesting or interested in them, at least smart people don't. Certainly it's fine to have your indiscretions, your flings, but marriage is a partnership—a sizing up of what each can bring to the table."

"How romantic," I said sarcastically.

"Romance is for fairy tales and the movies."

"Alan loves the movies."

"Alan Keyes, you're talking about," she stated sharply.

"Of course."

"He's that police officer that's helped you with your last couple of cases—the one you've been spending so much time with, the one you keep talking about."

"That would be the one, yes."

"Oh, honestly, Heath. I'm sure he's a nice boy, but he's a police officer. That's too close for comfort. I thought you said you were discreet."

"All I said was he loves the movies."

"And you've said before that he's quite handsome, and witty, and charming."

"All right, so what? So I like him. Is he what's brought all this on?"

She nodded. "He sounds like a movie star, too good to be true. He even has a movie star name. Have you ever noticed how people in the movies never have real names like Tom Lombrowski or Susan Klinghauefer?"

"Said the woman named Verbina," I said with a wry smile.

"That's enough cheek out of you for one day. In any case, he is most certainly sizing you up."

"Maybe I'm sizing him up, Auntie. I like his size."

Verbina glanced about the dining room and lowered her voice. "I won't have you talking like that, Heath. It's not decent."

"You'd like him if you got to know him."

She shook her head, and the plume waved back and forth again. "I don't like people as a rule, Heath. They always disappoint. And I don't want you to be hurt, to be disappointed. You're a police detective now, and you're starting to get some big cases. People are noticing you. Why, even my hairdresser mentioned you the other day."

"Because he knows I'm your nephew, and he likes your big tips."

"My what?" Her eyes grew wide and her face flushed.

"Tips, Auntie. T-i-p-s."

"Oh, yes, tips, of course. But it's not just that, my darling. You're going places. You could be the next commissioner if you wanted."

"I don't want to be the next commissioner. I'm happy where I am."

"Well, if you want to *stay* happy where you are, then find a nice girl. At least put up a front. If you want to be with your friend, fine. You know I don't judge, but do it discreetly."

"Live a lie? Would that be fair to her? To this girl you want me to find?"

"Always be true to yourself, Heath."

"But not to others?"

"Honesty isn't always what it's cracked up to be. The woman you select will be proud to be a detective's wife, Heath. You'll make her happy, perhaps have children. You'll give her a lovely home, security. That's all a woman wants."

"Is that all you wanted when you married your husbands?"

"Of course! I always married well and married up."

"I'm sorry, Aunt Bina, I can't do that."

"Honestly, Heath, sometimes I wonder. I'm not saying to give up your friend if this is someone you truly like, but that doesn't have to stop you from marriage, believe me. I've never told you, but my first husband, your uncle Michael, was that way. I knew about it almost immediately, and I truly didn't care. He gave me everything I ever wanted and he made me very happy."

I raised my eyebrows. "I must say I wondered about him."

"Only because you have a sense about men like that.

Most people never suspected. He provided me with a beautiful home, clothes, trips, a generous allowance, and I gave him respectability. Michael would have his little dalliances, of course, usually on Friday afternoons when I played bridge."

"You knew about them?"

"Of course I did, though I pretended not to, darling. It was all a game, you see. But eventually, we both got tired of playing it."

"He moved to San Francisco, didn't he?"

"Yes, but we keep in touch. When we divorced, he couldn't have been happier about it and neither could I. We're still the best of friends."

"And then you met David Partridge."

"That's right. A handsome devil, emphasis on the latter. I admit I was a bit smitten with him when we were first married, and the fact that he was a partner in a law firm didn't hurt."

"Nothing funny about him, I'd say."

She shook her head rather vehemently, and the red plume in her hat waved wildly about again. "Oh, he likes the ladies all right—too much."

"It bothered you more that he had lady friends than your first husband having men friends?"

"Yes, because David wasn't discreet. It became very public and ugly. When I found out, I got out, but only after I got what I needed. He didn't live up to his part of the bargain, you see. Romance really has nothing to do with it."

"I find that rather sad, Auntie."

"You can find it sad, but I'm very happy, and so are they now. Michael's a respectable divorced man sharing a two-bedroom flat with a nice chap, and David is on his third wife, I believe, or perhaps his fourth. My dear, all I really want for you is to be happy. I know how much your career means to you, but if you continue the way you're going and get discovered, you'll end up ruining your life. Is that what you want? What could this Alan Keyes possibly ever offer you that would make up for that?"

I drained my teacup and returned it to the saucer. "I don't know, Auntie. Maybe nothing. Maybe more than either of us knows. I don't know where this is going. It's all too new, but I want to explore it, and I will. I am. We're both scared about the future, about if we're doing the right thing, but he seems to really care for me the way I am."

"You can care for each other, but there's no reason you can't be married to a nice young girl, too."

I gazed at her, sitting there so sternly. "When Alan and I were in Lake Geneva together, we had a discussion along these lines. He talked about maybe wanting a family someday, kids and all."

"He sounds far more practical than you at the moment."

"I think he was scared. His second cousin Tony was found hanging from the rafters in some old barn after his father found out about him."

"Oh dear, how dreadful."

"Indeed. And besides being scared, I think he's afraid of dying alone."

"That, my dear, is inevitable."

"Maybe so, I don't know. We talked about you, too, Aunt Bina."

"Me?"

"Yes, about how you always say to live life to the fullest. Well, this is living life to the fullest for me—exploring, finding my way. If I can do it with Alan, so much the better."

She sat back, looking somewhat defeated. "I'm finished here, dear. I can see that. You might as well take me home. I'm playing bridge tonight with Mary Fiedler and the girls." She pulled on her gloves and picked up her pocketbook.

"I'm finished, too."

"I sincerely hope not, my dear boy. I hope you're just beginning. Promise me you'll at least think about what I've said."

"Yes, Aunt Bina, of course. And promise me you'll think about what I've said."

She looked at me sternly. "I shall have to meet this Mr. Keyes, I think."

I grinned back at her. "You'll like him a lot."

"If he makes you behave like a blooming idiot, there must be something to him. Now let's go, I can't be late for bridge."

I paid the check, collected my hat from the chair seat, and escorted her back into my old Buick once the valet had brought it around.

CHAPTER TWO

By the time I dropped Aunt Verbina back at her apartment and beat it back to my flat on Prospect Ave, it was after six. Dusk was approaching fast, but it was still light out. I found a spot under a streetlight for my trusty old bucket of rust and strode up the walk to my building. I let myself into the lobby, climbed the three flights of stairs, and crossed the hall to my apartment. Once inside, I took off my fedora, hung it on the rack next to the mirror in the hall, picked up the receiver of the telephone on the stand next to the mirror, and dialed the number for the station.

Doris answered. I could always tell it was her by the way she pronounced police, more like "po-lease department."

"Hey, Doris, it's Barrington. Any messages?"

"Hold on, let me look. I just got on duty." I heard her shuffling through papers. "Yes, sir. Chief wants to see you first thing in the morning, eight sharp."

I furrowed my brow. "What about?"

"Doesn't say."

"That's odd. Feinstein's on call tonight, not me, and Green's on for the weekend."

"I just pass along the messages, Detective."

"It's just puzzling, that's all. Can't it wait until nine, when I normally get in?"

"You know when the chief says eight sharp, he doesn't mean nine, Detective."

"Swell. I'll be in at eight. Try to keep any calls down tonight so I can get some rest, okay?"

"Sure thing, doll. Like you said, Feinstein's in the hot seat until the morning anyway."

Doris wasn't big on protocol, but I liked her. I hung up the phone and went into the bedroom, flicking on the overhead light, thankful I left all the windows open this morning and the manager had put up the screens already. The place was warm and stuffy. I couldn't stop wondering about what the chief wanted as I took off my suit coat and pulled down the roller shade on the window. I suppose something could have leaked about Alan and me, despite our discretion. I slipped off my tie, hanging it and my suit coat in the closet. Perhaps Alan had said something to someone he thought he could trust. I soon dismissed that notion, though. I hadn't known Alan long, but he had more sense than that. At least I thought he did.

I sat on the bed and took my shoes off, lining them up neatly on the closet floor next to the others. I slipped off the leather shoulder holster that held my service revolver and placed it in the nightstand next to my bed before undoing my collar, taking out my cufflinks, and rolling up my sleeves.

I made a quick trip to the bathroom and then flicked on the overhead light in the kitchen. It doesn't have a window, but it opens into the dining room, which has two large ones facing north. If I leaned out and looked east, I could just see the lake. I opened the icebox and rooted around for something to eat: an apple, some leftover chili, a quart of milk, some butter, a couple bottles of pop, and some eggs. Lean pickings.

I decided on a couple of fried eggs and the chili, heating up the chili in one pan and frying the eggs in the other. From the vent in the wall next to the stove, I heard the unmistakable voice of Mrs. Murphy downstairs in 204. "Herbert! I've almost got the dishes done—do you want to see a movie? The Downer has *Unconquered* starring Gary Cooper at eight fifteen, what about that? The theater has refrigerated air, you know." She had a set of lungs on her, that's for sure. Funny, the few times I've run into Mr. Murphy in the hall, he didn't seem hard of hearing.

"Fine, just sit there, then, and listen to the radio and sweat. That's all you ever want to do. Maybe I'll call my sister and go with her. She likes Gary Cooper."

"Who doesn't like Gary Cooper?" I said to myself. I turned off the stove, dished the eggs onto a plate and the chili into a bowl, and carried them to the table in the dining room, which was really more of an alcove off the living room. When I went back for a bottle of pop I heard Mrs. Murphy once again.

"I'm going to catch the streetcar and meet Evelyn there. I just have time to change my dress. If you'd come with, we could take the car, you know, and I wouldn't have to rush." I suspected Mr. Murphy was going to enjoy the peace and quiet of being home alone in spite of the heat.

As for me, my place was too quiet. Even Oscar, Mrs. Ferguson's cat in 310, wasn't roaming about yet. She usually let him out in the hall around eight, and he went from door to door looking for love and affection. Sometimes I hated living alone, especially when I started envying a cat. I sat down and started eating, staring at the phone over by the door and wishing I could call Alan and talk to him about all this right now, but he was on patrol until midnight. Instead I turned my attention to the dining room windows and the ever-deepening twilight. I pondered over and over what the chief could want to see me about. I would have a restless night of worrying, tossing and turning. I also wondered what Keyes was doing right now and if he was thinking of me.

CHAPTER THREE

The alarm went off at six the next morning, and I pulled myself unwillingly out of bed. As I suspected, I did not sleep well. A hot shower, a shave, and some breakfast and I felt well enough to make a call to Alan Keyes's apartment. I used the pencil on the table to dial the phone, holding my second cup of coffee in my other hand. After five rings, I heard a sleepy "hullo?"

"Hey, sleepyhead."

"Heath, geez, it's six thirty in the morning. What are you doing up this early?"

"I've got business. The chief wants to see me at eight. Sorry to wake you."

"S'okay. I didn't get done on patrol until midnight, though, and didn't get to bed until almost two."

"Good thing you're young yet."

"I won't be if you don't let me get some rest."

"Sorry, I guess I should have waited to call. I just wanted to say good morning. We didn't get to talk last night."

I heard Alan yawn. "What's he want to see you about?"

"Dunno. I've been thinking about it all night. Didn't get much sleep."

"Probably just an upcoming case. Nothing to worry about, I'm sure."

"Yeah, you're probably right, Alan. There's nothing going on right now that I know of, but I'll keep you posted. I told him we're going fishing, so he already approved me being off."

"I know. Say, you don't suppose he's heard anything. About us, I mean."

I shuddered at the thought, Verbina's words ringing in my ears. "Funny you bring that up. I was wondering the same thing. I don't see how, though. We've been pretty discreet. Nothing wrong with two buddies hanging out together, going fishing for the weekend."

"Except you're a detective and I'm a cop. Detectives usually keep to their own," Alan replied.

"Usually, but not always. We've worked on a couple of cases together, it's natural we should become friends. I'm sure whatever he wants to see me about is nothing personal."

Alan let out a deep breath. "Let me know when you find out."

"I will. Say, you didn't by chance say anything to anyone about us, did you? One of the guys downtown, maybe?"

"What? Are you kidding? You should know me better than that, especially after all the stories you've told me." The indignation in his voice made me instantly regret asking him.

"I'm sorry. I didn't think you would have, but I had to ask."

"I don't see why you had to ask that, Heath. I have just as much to lose as you do if someone finds out about us."

"I'm sorry. I guess I'm just nervous."

"I understand you're nervous, but I didn't say anything to anybody, and I never would. He may want to ask about a case or one of your files. Aren't you working on some larceny case right now?"

"Petty larceny. Nothing big that couldn't wait until nine. But you're right. It's probably nothing, and soon we'll be on our way to a three-day weekend up north."

"We both could use it. It will be nice to get away, Heath, I've been looking forward to it for weeks. I work tonight at four, but I'll be done by midnight, and I'll see you tomorrow morning. I still can't believe you managed to arrange for both of us to be off Decoration Day, and it's on a Friday this year, so three days off."

"Most folks call it Memorial Day now, not Decoration Day, and it wasn't easy to get us off. I had to call a few favors in, pull some strings."

"Well, I'm glad you did. Our last weekend away in Lake Geneva wasn't exactly relaxing."

I laughed. "No, not exactly. I got my man, but not the one I wanted."

"No murders this time. Just the two of us alone, in a cabin by the lake."

"Sounds good to me, Alan. Don't forget to bring your fishing pole."

Alan laughed. "I've never fished a day in my life, but I'll bring my bait along."

"Perfect. What are you wearing, by the way?"

"Just my boxers at the moment, but I may as well get dressed. I'm up now."

"Don't bother on my account."

He laughed again. "What are you wearing?"

"Just my boxers, too."

"Really?"

"Yeah, but I'll also be getting dressed soon."

"Too bad."

"Sweet talker. So glad police officers and detectives have private phone lines."

"Maybe someday they'll invent picture phones."

"Now that would be nice!"

"I'll pick you up tomorrow morning at nine. It's a three-hour drive up there, so we'll get in in time for lunch."

"Great. I get off at midnight tonight, so if I'm home and in bed by one, I should be able to get seven hours in, *if* you don't call me before eight."

"No worries, sunshine, I won't. But if you're not out front at nine, I'll be beeping my horn."

"I'll be there, Detective, you can count on it. Let me know what the chief says, okay?"

"I'll give you a call after I've finished with him."

"Good, and don't worry about it anymore. See you later, Heath."

"Bye, Officer."

I hung up and swallowed the rest of the now-cold coffee before padding down the hall to my bedroom. I put on my navy blue pinstripe suit with the yellow tie, shoulder harness under the coat, grabbed my hat from the hook, and headed downstairs. On the second-floor landing, I passed the milkman making his rounds and looking sharp in his white shirt and coat, black slacks, and black bow tie. I asked him to leave me a pint of cottage cheese the next morning. He jotted it down, and I continued on my way downstairs.

Mrs. Murphy was in the lobby, standing with her back to me in front of the bank of brass mailboxes in the wall. Her hair was up in a kerchief, which did little to disguise a mound of curlers beneath it, and she was wearing a housedress with colorful vertical stripes. In Mrs. Murphy's case, the vertical stripes definitely did not make her look thinner.

"Good morning, Mrs. Murphy."

She turned around, a startled look on her chubby face, and I saw she'd been reading a postcard, probably left on the ledge for someone else. "Oh, Mr. Barrington, you startled me. You shouldn't sneak up on old ladies like that."

"My apologies, but you're hardly an old lady." I grinned at her.

Her cheeks flushed a soft pink, and she giggled. "Oh, go on, you flatterer!"

"Not at all. I swear you look younger every day. You're certainly up bright and early, by the way."

"It's too hot to sleep in, Mr. Barrington. And Herbert is a furnace himself. I had to get up and sleep on the davenport."

"It was pretty warm last night." I took the opportunity to check my own mailbox and was pleased to find a letter from my friend David, a Catholic missionary stationed in Africa, of all places, and a postcard from my aunt and uncle. They were vacationing in Margate, New Jersey, home of Lucy the Elephant, which apparently weighed ninety tons and was sixty-five feet tall and made of wood, according to the description on the back.

"You got a postcard, too?" Mrs. Murphy said, trying her best to see it.

"Yes, a letter and a postcard of Lucy the Elephant in New Jersey. Alan would get a kick out of that." I placed the letter and the postcard in my inside pocket to show him later.

"Who's Alan?"

"Hmmm, oh, just someone at the station who likes things like big wooden elephants. By the way, how was *The Conqueror*?"

"Why, it was wonderful, but how did you know? Oh yes, the vent, of course. I do need to be careful of what I say lest you learn all my secrets!" She giggled again.

"Your secrets are safe with me, Mrs. Murphy. I'm glad you enjoyed the show."

"Oh yes, very much so. Gary Cooper, you know, and air-conditioning. Refrigerated air—it was heavenly. We missed the newsreel because we had to take the streetcar, but we got to see the shorts and the coming attractions before the movie. Mr. Cooper is so dreamy." Her eyes sparkled and she tittered, covering her mouth with the postcard, which I could now see was addressed to Alice McBain.

"He's a fine actor indeed. One of my favorites. I see Miss McBain got a postcard."

"Hmm? Oh, yes!" She turned the postcard over in her hand, rather embarrassed. "It was lying here on the ledge. The sender didn't put her apartment number on it, you know. I was just going to take it up and slip it under her door."

"Very kind of you."

"Oh, it's nothing, really. I pass her door anyway when I go up. Poor Alice. Her beau was killed in the war, so tragic. They were engaged, you know."

"Yes, I recall you mentioning that."

"Now she just sits home all alone most nights. She still wears her engagement ring."

"How sad."

"Yes, it truly is. She works at the bank during the day, then comes home by herself at night. The card is from her cousin Shirley out in Minneapolis, the one that just had twins."

"I see."

"Well, not that I read it or anything, but I saw the postmark and the signature."

"Of course. That makes perfect sense."

"Well, anyway, I take it you were home alone again last night, too, seeing as how you heard me and the mister through the vent and all."

"Yes, a quiet evening. Just me and the radio."

"You spend too many nights with that radio, Mr. B," she admonished. "A nice, young, handsome man like yourself should be going out and enjoying yourself. You're always working or sitting home alone, just like Miss McBain." She fanned herself with the postcard. "Oh my, it's going to be a warm one again today."

"Yes, I believe it is."

"It's too early in the year for weather like this. Terrible sleeping. Now mark my words, you need to find yourself some pretty young thing and get married, Mr. Barrington. Then when you stay home, you'll have something better to do than listen to the radio." Her face flushed pink again. "And don't forget Miss McBain, such a nice girl and all alone now, you know."

"Yes, Mrs. Murphy, so you've said." *A dozen or more times*, I added to myself. "Well, I must be off. I have to get to work."

"At least tomorrow is Decoration Day, or Memorial Day, as they're calling it these days. Herbert and I will be going to the cemetery with flowers, decorating the graves of the soldiers. That's how Decoration Day got its name, you know."

"Yes, I'm aware of that, but somehow Memorial Day seems a more fitting, more somber name."

"I suppose so. Everything changes, don't it? I suppose you have to work the holiday, too?"

"Police work never takes a holiday, you know, but I'm supposed to be off tomorrow and the whole weekend."

Her chubby cheeks glowed. "Oh, how nice for you! Any plans? Will you be going to the cemetery and the parade later?"

"Not this year, Mrs. Murphy. I'm going fishing up north with a buddy—we've rented a cabin on a lake."

"Oh, that sounds nice. But it's too bad, really."

"Why?" I said, though I knew I shouldn't have.

"I was just thinking, the VFW hall is having a dance Saturday night and it would be nice if you were to ask Miss McBain. She's mentioned how attractive you are, you know, and I'm sure you're a good dancer. Herbert and I are planning on going, too. We could double date."

I resisted the urge to roll my eyes. "I'm afraid I'm better with a pole than on a dance floor, and as I said, I've already made plans. I really have to get going or I'll be late, Mrs. Murphy. Give my best to Mr. Murphy." I stepped around her and headed for the door as Mrs. Murphy tsked behind me. I imagined she was shaking her head at me, still fanning herself with the purloined postcard.

CHAPTER FOUR

It was almost eight when I entered the stiflingly hot detectives' briefing room. The fan overhead did little more than move the air around, which I guess was something. In the corner, a nasty-looking fly strip twirled lazily in the breeze, its victims stuck to it like absurd little ornaments. I paced, watching the clock on the wall, still wondering and worrying what this could all be about.

I stopped briefly at the open window and looked down on Eighth Street, watching people and cars crawling slowly along. Funny thing about summers and heat. They make everything move at a different pace. In the winter, people almost hibernate, and those that do venture out are almost unrecognizable bundled up in coats, hats, scarves, and earmuffs as they scurry quickly about. In the summertime the heat brings everyone outdoors to their porches and their stoops, drinking lemonade and saying howdy to passersby.

Summertime is a friendlier season, but this was still technically spring and it was too damned hot. I turned from the window and sat down in an uncomfortable wooden chair against the wall, picking up a *Saturday Evening Post* from a stack of old magazines to fan myself with as I fiddled with my tie, a nervous habit.

I jumped when the chief finally walked in, looking more than a little warm and tired himself.

"Morning," he said to me.

"Good morning, sir." I rose to my feet and dropped the magazine back onto the table next to the chair.

"Am I late?"

I glanced at the large clock on the wall over the door. Eleven after. "Only a little."

The chief looked at the clock, then back at me, and shrugged. "Overslept. Too damned hot, and if we leave the windows open in the bedroom, we get eaten alive."

"You haven't put your screens in yet?"

He glowered at me. "Don't you start in on me, too. My wife's been nagging me to get the storms off and the screens put in for the last two days, but I've been busy. I got the first floor done, but not the upstairs."

"The upstairs windows are always challenging. You have to be careful on those ladders."

"Don't I know it, damned things. It's too early in the year for it to be this hot already."

"I know. Tune in tomorrow—it will probably snow."

The chief laughed gruffly. "Exactly, and then she'll want me to put the storms back on. It was in the forties and fifties just last week. And don't forget January was just four months ago, with the blizzard that left us with eighteen inches of snow, sixty-mile-an-hour winds, and drifts over ten feet high."

"Yeah, and now we're complaining about the heat. Human nature."

"Come on in, Barrington." He unlocked the door to his office and I followed him in, closing it behind me. I hung my fedora on the coat rack next to his and dragged a wooden chair across the already badly scuffed linoleum on the opposite side of his desk.

I watched him as he turned on the fan in the corner, opened the windows, and finally sat down at his desk, where he sorted through his papers, made a few notes, and grunted to himself. After several minutes, he lit a cigarette and looked up at me, his eyes bloodshot and his forehead beaded with sweat.

"I suppose you're wondering why I wanted you down here first thing."

I shrugged, watching him, hoping my nerves didn't show. "I'm curious, of course." My stomach was in knots, as I had worked out the worst-case scenario in my head, involving me losing my job, public humiliation, my parents shunning me.

At last he said, "I've got an assignment for you, on a need-to-know basis only. I couldn't give any details in the message."

I sighed heavily, quite relieved. Sometimes my imagination is my own worst enemy. "Oh, so that's it."

"Why? What did you think I wanted?"

"I wasn't sure, really. What kind of assignment?"

"It's probably nothing, Barrington, but we can't take the chance. Gregor Slavinsky's on the move again, or he's going to be, anyway." He picked up a manila folder and slid it across the desk to me.

I picked it up and leafed through it, feeling as though a huge weight had been lifted from my shoulders. Gregor Slavinsky was a small-town thug, in and out of prison like it had a revolving door on it. He'd just been released the middle of February on a racketeering charge. He was someone we kept tabs on, hoping he'd lead us to bigger fish.

"What's he up to this time?"

The chief grimaced. "Wish we knew. Word is he's into Benny Ballentine for big bucks, somewhere in the neighborhood of twenty-five grand."

I whistled, rocking back on the legs of the wooden chair, which creaked accordingly. Benny Ballentine was definitely a bigger fish we'd been trying to hook for years. The two of them had been bootleggers together back in the twenties, though Ballentine had gone on to a more lucrative life of crime while Slavinsky struggled every step of the way and spent more time in prison than out. "Ballentine still playing the part of the legitimate businessman these days?"

"Yes. He owns quite a bit of property and several businesses and nightclubs downtown, many of which we suspect are fronts for gambling and prostitution, but we haven't been able to nail him. Gregor's booked passage on a lake excursion boat leaving this afternoon, and our sources tell us Ballentine's going along."

"Interesting," I said, rocking back and forth.

"Very."

"Why would Ballentine let Slavinsky have 25 Gs? That's a lot of money, and from what I hear, Slavinsky is not a good risk for a loan."

"Good question. Our contact tells us it was a high-interest loan Slavinsky had planned to use to open a nightclub downtown, but apparently he's having problems and has already missed a payment to Ballentine."

"Ouch. Benny Ballentine doesn't like missed payments."

The chief shook his head. "No, he doesn't. My guess is Ballentine doesn't want Gregor slipping away into Canada until he gets his money, so he's tagging along on this trip to keep an eye on him. The boat's some small four-cabin excursion yacht sailing from Milwaukee down to Chicago and then up to Mackinac Island, over to Beaver Island on Saturday, and stopping in Manitowoc on Sunday, returning to Milwaukee on Sunday afternoon. The only other passengers are some folks from Chicago—a man by the name of Alex Baines Whitaker and, apparently, Whitaker's aunt, a Mrs. Vivian Woodfork. They booked a cabin together."

"So Gregor's got a cabin, Whitaker and his aunt have a cabin, and Ballentine's got one."

"Along with his thug, George, yeah. Leaving one cabin empty."

I brought my chair down to rest on all fours and leaned on the desk. "And you want me to occupy that empty cabin."

The chief grinned. "You are definitely a smart one, Barrington, just like the reporters say. Shirley booked you under the name Henry Benson. You're an insurance salesman on holiday." He slid another folder across at me. "Here's all the info and your ticket."

I picked it up. "Leaving this afternoon? So I'll be gone all weekend?"

"Like I said, the boat returns Sunday afternoon. It's taking a leisurely route, a tour of the lake, more or less. It leaves here at six tonight, getting to Chicago at seven thirty, leaves there at eight and arrives in Mackinac at eight tomorrow morning."

"That is a leisurely route. You can drive there from here in eight or nine hours."

"Apparently, this boat isn't in it for speed. They serve meals on board and everything, I guess, just like a hotel. All your expenses will be paid, of course. You'll be home by Sunday night."

"And what exactly am I supposed to be doing on this trip? Once we get out into the lake, I'll be out of our jurisdiction. Shouldn't this be the Feds' department? Crossing state lines and all?"

"No crime has been committed yet, and Slavinsky has served his time, so he's free to travel wherever he wants. That being said, Slavinsky borrowed money, and Ballentine wants it back."

"So, you want me to tag along in case Ballentine decides to get persuasive."

"Exactly. I'd love to bust Ballentine for murder one, if I can—attempted murder at the very least."

I nodded. "And if Ballentine bumps off Slavinsky, you have one less headache to worry about. Killing two birds with one stone, as they say."

"I know that sounds cold, Barrington. I don't want Slavinsky killed, but if it happens, it happens. I just want you to nail Ballentine if it *does* happen." The chief took a long drag on his cigarette and blew the smoke toward another fly strip hanging in the corner opposite the fan.

"Sure, Chief. I understand."

"Good. I doubt much of anything will happen when you're out on the water, but keep your eyes and ears open at all times."

"I'll do my best. What about on land? It will be difficult to tail them."

"I doubt Slavinsky will make a run for the border once he finds out Ballentine is aboard, but you never know. Contact the state police in Michigan if you need help. They've been briefed on the situation. The Canadian border police have been briefed as well, just in case, and we sent them mug shots of Slavinsky and Ballentine."

"I understand."

"The state police will meet the boat in Mackinac just in case Slavinsky makes a run for it."

"But even if he does, it's not a crime to go to Canada."

"No, but if he runs, you can bet Ballentine will follow, or he wouldn't be on this boat with him. He wants his money back, and he'll do what it takes. If Slavinsky runs and Ballentine follows, go after them with the Michigan State Police, but keep your distance. As soon as Ballentine pulls something, nail him but good."

"Okay, Chief. And I should just lay low on board, the average insurance salesman on holiday?"

"Ask around a bit while you cruise. See if you can find out what Gregor has done with all that money so far, or anything we could hold Ballentine on. But yeah, otherwise just sit back and relax with your eyes and ears open. You could get worse assignments, Barrington, though I know you had that fishing trip planned." He stubbed out his cigarette in a dirty glass ashtray and fanned his face with one of the folders.

"Had being the key word. What about Alvin Green? He's the senior detective and on call this weekend."

"You're right, and we need him here in case something big happens in town. As I said, we really don't expect much of anything to go down with Gregor and Ballentine, and we can't have Green out in the middle of the lake if something big occurs here." The chief wiped the back of his neck with his handkerchief. "Besides, Green's a family man. He needs time to spend with the family."

Aunt Verbina flashed through my mind again, and I felt a chill run down my spine. "Right," I replied, bristling.

"Oh, I almost forgot. Speaking of families, here's yours for the weekend." He slid an envelope across the desk toward me. "Wife, a boy and a girl, standard stuff. Insurance agents your age would naturally be married."

"Naturally." I took the envelope and opened it to reveal a small photo of a woman and two attractive children, the boy in her arms, the girl in a white dress by her side.

"Put that in your wallet. You can name them whatever you want, but don't forget. The back story is your wife took the kids to visit her mother in Minnesota, and you decided to take a lake cruise, got it?"

I put the photo back in the envelope and slid it inside one of the files. "Got it. Attractive woman and kids, anyway."

The chief laughed as he lit up yet another cigarette. "You're a nice-looking guy, or so my wife tells me. She keeps wanting to fix you up. We can't have a nice-looking guy married to an old hag, wouldn't be believable."

"Thanks. Why didn't I go with her to visit her mother?"

"Good question. You're also a bit of a Great Lakes buff, and you've always wanted to do a trip like this, but your wife gets seasick, and you're not all that keen on her mother. There's some facts and figures on the lake in the folder for you to memorize, too."

"Couldn't I just be single? Or divorced? Or a widower? Seems it would be a lot simpler."

"A guy like you would be married. You're too young to be a widower, and divorce isn't believable. Oh yeah, you'll need this." He opened his top drawer and took out another envelope, which he slid across to me. Inside was a gold wedding band. I slipped it on my ring finger, and it fit pretty well.

"Don't lose that. We'll need it back on Monday morning."

"Don't worry, I don't plan on keeping it." I took it off and put it securely in my front pocket. "What about my larceny case? The MacDonald/Henning one?"

"That can wait until Monday. It's not going anywhere."

"Right. Well, I guess I'd better study these files and do some packing."

"Don't forget you'll be out of communication once you leave land, but the boat is equipped with ship-to-shore radio in case of an emergency. The captain's a fellow named Clark and the mate is a man by the name of Willy Gruling. They seem to be on the up-and-up, but don't trust anyone. There's also a cook on board, some fellow by the name of Gene Gidlund. Been with them a long time. And we have an undercover policeman name of Grant Riker acting as steward."

I raised my eyebrows. "An undercover policeman and an undercover detective on one little boat?"

"You know we've been after Benny Ballentine for years.

We can't afford to let him slip away while our back is turned. It would be a real coup for Milwaukee if we can pull this off and nail him."

"So what's Riker's story? Does he know I'll be aboard?"

"Not yet, but he'll be filled in. He's on the boat now, learning the ropes, so to speak. We felt we needed someone who could get into all the cabins and snoop about a bit, and we need you to be with Ballentine and Gregor in the public areas, chatting, listening, watching."

"Makes sense, I suppose. A room steward would have the perfect opportunity to snoop without suspicion."

"Exactly. We chose Riker because he had experience as a steward while he was in school a couple years ago, and we arranged for the current steward to be sick for this voyage."

It never failed to surprise me how much the police could arrange when necessary, and I didn't always want to know how. "How long have you known about all this?"

He brought his big bushy eyebrows together. "Gregor booked passage a week or so ago, according to our contacts. Ballentine shortly after that. Sorry for the short notice on your end, but we had to put everything together first."

"Got it. I guess I'll see you Monday, then."

"Right. You can always go fishing another time."

I nodded. "Sure, sure. They probably aren't biting anyway, unlike these flies." I swatted at and missed a black fly that had thus far eluded the fly strip in the corner.

He exhaled a puff of smoke. "Have a safe trip, and study those files before you board. The necessary paperwork and identification materials are in there, too."

I got to my feet and tucked the files under my arm. "Will do, Chief." I grabbed my hat from the coat rack and left his office, my heart heavy. I stopped at my desk, filled out some paperwork, looked briefly through the dossiers the chief had given me, and perused the brochure for the trip, done in two colors, trifolded.

I knew I should read it all over carefully, but I couldn't concentrate. I kept thinking about Alan, knowing I had to call and tell him our trip was off, as much as I hated to. I picked up the phone on my desk a few times but thought better of it. Too much of a chance of being overheard here. Finally, I grabbed my hat and headed out the door, leaving word with the desk sergeant as to where I would be and letting him know I'd check in. I took the stairs down slowly and went out the side door, the heat hitting me like an oven the moment I stepped onto Eighth street. I left my car in the lot and headed down the street on foot, my fedora shading my eyes from the bright morning sun.

CHAPTER FIVE

Fowler Drug was on the corner of Ninth and State, just down from the station, and a short walk. I pushed open the glass door and stepped inside just as the clock struck ten over at the courthouse. It was a small drugstore, clean and neat: a few rows of shelves, a pharmacy counter at the back, and a soda fountain along the far wall. The air smelled faintly antiseptic, moved about by four large ceiling fans spinning slightly off center.

The phone booth near the front door was unoccupied. I pushed open the wood and glass bifold door and stepped inside, pulling it closed behind me. What is it with phone booths? They all have that same rather foul odor, a mix between stale cigarettes and a men's washroom. Maybe I didn't want to know. The phone book hung down from a metal chain, and it swung back and forth, rapping against my knees as I fished in my pockets for a nickel and dropped it into the slot. My father always taught me to carry certain things in my trouser pockets: a pocketknife, a comb, a small pencil, and loose change. I listened as the coin plunked down into the repository and then dialed Alan's number. As I listened to it ring, I noticed someone had scratched "D.S.P. + A.A.K." inside a heart into the paint on the side of the phone. Defacing private property.

"Hello?"

"Hey you, it's Heath. I'm calling from a phone booth in Fowler's."

"Hey there! What's up? I've been waiting for your call. I couldn't even get back to sleep. What did the chief have to say?"

"The good news is it wasn't anything personal."

"That's very good news. I've been worried about it all morning."

"I know, me too."

"So, what's the bad news?"

"Our fishing trip is off."

"You're joking."

"I wish I were here. I'm really sorry, Alan."

"Damn it, Heath, I've been looking forward to this for weeks. You got us the time off, everything. Why is it off? What's happened?"

I sighed. "I'm sorry, I really am. The chief has an assignment for me, on a need-to-know basis only, very last minute."

"Meaning you can't even tell me what it's about or why our fishing trip is off."

"Sorry, no. It's nothing major, though. I have to go to Mackinac, and I won't be back until Sunday afternoon."

"Mackinac? As in Michigan? You don't have any jurisdiction there."

"Yeah, I know. I can't really explain it right now, it's kind of complicated."

"If I had to guess, I would say he wants you to escort a prisoner."

"That's a pretty good guess, but not exactly."

"I see. So, that's it, then? We're not going on our trip?"

"No. Like I said, I'm sorry, Alan, honestly. I'm disappointed, too."

"I'm all packed, figures."

"I'd rather go away with you, you know that."

"Would you? I wonder sometimes."

"Of course I would. I was looking forward to this just as much as you were, you know that."

"Couldn't you have just said no? The chief had already approved your time. We have all these plans, the cabin..."

"I couldn't just say no. This is my job, it's important."

"Of course. You're a detective. Your job, your cases, are more important than anything else."

I sighed. "You're being unreasonable. Of course you're important, too, but we'll have other weekends, other trips."

"Sure, Heath. What about Green? I thought he was on call this weekend."

"He is, but this is a special case they want me for. They need Green in town. Besides, Green has a wife and kids. I'm single."

He laughed harshly. "Yeah, I guess so."

"I'm sorry. We'll plan something else when I get back."

"And then something else will come up."

"You don't understand. I'm just getting started on some big cases. I need to focus on my job. You're just a policeman, you don't have to think about these kinds of things."

"Right. As long as you have your priorities straight. You're a big detective and I'm just a policeman."

"That's not what I meant. I have my career to think about, Alan. My future."

"And what about my future?"

I didn't say anything for probably too long. "We've only known each other a short time."

"That's true, and you're a detective and I'm just a policeman, like you said."

"Geez, it's not like I wanted to go to Mackinac, you know."

"Yeah, sure. But you couldn't say no, I understand."

"Look, you've got the time off, do something fun."

"Yeah, by myself. Fun. I guess I'll go to Haffensteffer's bachelor party tonight. The guys asked me to go. I wasn't planning on it, obviously, told them I had other plans, but now I guess I will."

"A bachelor party? You're kidding."

"No, Haffensteffer's getting married."

"Who's Haffensteffer?"

"Just a policeman. You wouldn't know him, being a detective and all."

I sighed again. "I've heard the name, probably saw him. There are a lot of men on the force."

"Yeah, I know. And you detectives live in your own world. As I said before, detectives keep to their own."

"Hey, come on, that's not fair. I was a policeman for many years, and I know the flatfoots keep to themselves just as much."

"True. That invisible line between the detectives and the guys in blue. And tonight, you'll be on your way to Mackinac and I'll be at the stag party. Not exactly what I was expecting."

"Yeah, I know. Me either. I suppose you should probably go to the party, though. Keep 'em from talking."

"Apparently, I'll have nothing better to do."

"I'm sorry, Alan, I really am."

"So you've said, several times. Look, you'd better hang up, I'm sure you've got lots to do before you leave, and this isn't a secured line."

"Yeah, I suppose so. Go to the stag party and have a good time."

"I'll go. A good time remains to be seen. Heath, are you sure you didn't say yes to this assignment because you got cold feet about us going away together?"

"Why would I do that? What would I have to be nervous about?"

"About someone finding out, of course."

"Everyone thinks we're going fishing, just a couple of buds."

"Fishing stinks, and so does this whole arrangement. Lying to everyone, sneaking around, hiding."

"We don't have a choice, Alan."

"Well, you certainly made yours. I can't help but wonder if things would be different if the chief knew you were planning on going away for the weekend with a girl."

"I wouldn't be going away for the weekend with a girl, Alan. It wouldn't be proper unless we were chaperoned or married."

"Yeah, but somehow I think the chief would see it differently. Look, I gotta go. I work tonight, and I have things to do yet."

"Tell Haffensteffer best of luck."

"Yeah, I'll do that. I'll call and cancel the cabin, though we'll probably lose our deposit."

"I'll pay you back the two bucks, and I'll try and call from Mackinac, if I can."

"If you want, and if you feel you won't be overheard. Just don't call too early. I may be out late."

I grimaced. "Understood."

"Well, see ya."

"See ya." I exited the phone booth and walked over to the soda fountain counter, my heart heavier than before. I stopped briefly at the nickelodeon and used my last nickel to play the saddest songs I could find, two for five cents, feeling miserably sorry for myself. I guess I expected, or hoped, Alan would be more understanding, or at least not as upset as he seemed to be. As the sad refrain started up from the jukebox, I settled on one of the red leather stools, putting my fedora on the empty stool to my left. I used my handkerchief to wipe my brow as I perused the menu hanging over the back counter.

"Yes, sir?" The soda jerk, in his crisp white uniform, black bow tie, and cap was looking at me from behind the counter. His name badge read Edgar.

"Chocolate egg cream, please."

"Yes, sir." He turned and set to work as I watched. Funny thing about egg creams: they aren't made with eggs or cream, but rather just chocolate syrup, milk, and seltzer. He finished up and brought it over to me in a nice tall glass, along with a nice tall bill for ten cents. I know for a fact I can get an egg cream at Hayek's on Downer for eight cents, but I wasn't going to argue. Besides, the jerk was kind of cute, if a little young. I was admiring his profile and still wallowing in self-pity when I heard a soft feminine voice over my left shoulder.

"Excuse me, but aren't you Heath Barrington?"

I swiveled around in my stool and found a very attractive young blonde. I looked her up and down before replying.

"Yes, that's right. Do I know you?"

She smiled shyly. "You probably don't remember me. We went to high school together, the last year anyway. My family moved here from Wausau my senior year. I'm Rosemary Adams."

"Rosemary, of course! Gee, you look so grown up now." And she did, too. Her hourglass figure was wrapped in a red polka-dot dress, and she wore red heels with white bows and a white-brimmed hat with a red band, her blond hair in long curls.

Rosemary laughed. "We all grow up, I suppose. I hope

I'm not disturbing you. It's just that I saw your picture in the paper a while ago, and well, I'm so glad I ran into you. I work in the millinery department at Schuster's. I just stopped in here for some aspirin before I go to work."

I got to my feet, remembering my manners too late. "Well, I'm glad you did. Would you like to join me for an egg cream? I could use a friendly face about now."

"I'd love to, and I'll put my best friendly face on. You do look pretty down in the dumps." She sat to my right, my hat still on the stool to my left, and I made myself comfortable back in the middle.

"Another egg cream for the lady, please." The jerk nodded and set to work as Rosemary turned to me.

"Did you put this music on?"

I nodded. "Uh-huh."

"Blue songs for a blue fellow. Care to talk about it?"

"I don't think so."

She smiled. "I understand. Goodness, it certainly is warm again today, isn't it, Heath?" she said, changing the subject.

"Yes, but I heard there's a chance of showers tonight."

"We could use it. My uncle Ralph up in Wausau is a farmer. It's been so dry this spring."

"I'll keep my fingers crossed for rain, then. Gee, I haven't seen you in nearly fifteen years. What have you been up to? Married? Kids?"

She shook her head, and her blond curls danced with the movement. "I'm not married. I was seeing Joe Schmidt, remember him? He was on the basketball team at school."

"Of course, Joe on the go."

"Yes, indeed, and he always was. We dated off and on while he went to college, then he started at his father's automobile dealership for a few years, and then the war..."

"Oh, I see. Don't tell me..."

She nodded. "He enlisted right after Pearl Harbor. I saw him once the following Christmas in '42, and that was it. We had talked about getting married, but he wanted to wait until he had more money and we could buy a house, do it right."

"I'm very sorry, Rosemary."

She smiled a rather melancholy, tired smile. "So am I, but life goes on, I go on, we all go on. It's been almost five years now."

"Doesn't make it any easier."

"No, it doesn't. Wounds heal but the scars remain." Then suddenly she laughed. "Gee, I was supposed to be putting on a happy face for you."

I smiled. "It's okay. It's nice just to talk to someone, someone who's not mad at me."

"Uh-oh. Girl troubles? Is that what's bothering you?"

I shrugged and nodded uncomfortably. "You know how it is sometimes."

"Of course." She touched my arm and looked at me softly. "I'm sure it's nothing too serious, and if you change your mind and want to talk about it, I'm all ears."

The jerk brought over her egg cream, and I was happy for the distraction.

"It's nothing too serious. We've only been seeing each other a couple of months. Our first fight, I guess, if you can call it that."

"Ah, I see. What's her name?"

"Uh, Ellen, she's uh, a secretary at the station," I lied, and I knew I was terrible at it.

"Ellen. That's a pretty name. I'm sure you'll smooth things over, and if not, there are lots of other girls, you know." She smiled at me as she sipped her egg cream.

"That's very true, Rosemary, very true indeed."

"I think it's so interesting that you're a police detective, Heath, I really do. And a handsome one, too."

I blushed. "And you're in the millinery department at Schuster's, and very pretty."

She laughed, tossing her hair to the side. "That's sweet of you. Working at Schuster's isn't that interesting, but I get a nice discount."

"That helps, I'm sure."

"It doesn't hurt when a girl likes to shop."

I smiled. "And girls do like to shop. No boyfriend?"

She shrugged. "No one serious. Men are in short supply right now, you know, at least eligible ones. I'm surprised no one's snatched you up yet."

"I'm kind of married to my job. It's no fun being the wife of a police detective."

"Oh, I don't know. Being a police detective is quite respectable, and there'd be a nice house in the country, a couple of kids, a big dog—there are worse things."

"Have you been talking to my Aunt Verbina?"

She laughed and wrinkled her nose. "Who's that?"

"Just someone you remind me of, in a way. My mother's sister."

"I hope that's a compliment."

"It is. I admire her a lot. She thinks I should be married, too."

"I see. Well, maybe I can meet her one day."

"She'd like you a lot, I can tell."

"I'm sure I'd like her a lot, too, Heath." She swiveled on her barstool, her egg cream just about gone.

"Well, it's been really swell catching up, Rosemary, but I had better get going. I have plans for the weekend, and it's after eleven already."

"Oh, that's too bad—that you have to get going, I mean. I hope I can see you again."

"Sure, sure. May I walk you to the streetcar?"

"Oh, no thank you. I still have to get my aspirin and a few other things. I don't start work until noon. Listen, I still live with my mother, she's in the book. Call me sometime, huh?"

"Well, uh, sure, Rosemary, sure. How is your mother?"

"Oh, she's fine. She's a great cook. Maybe you can come for dinner sometime, I mean, if things don't work out with that Ellen."

Aunt Verbina flashed through my mind again. *You should be married.* "I appreciate that, and I'll keep it in mind."

"It looks like you could use a good home-cooked meal, Heath. Mom's in the book, like I said, or you can find me at Schuster's most days except Tuesdays and Sundays."

"Got it."

"The music's over, Heath. No more sad songs, okay?"

I smiled. "Deal. Anyway, take care of yourself, Rosemary. You really do look swell." I stood up, leaving a quarter on the counter to cover our egg creams and the tip, and I gave her a peck on the cheek. She smelled like roses.

"Thanks, Heath, you too. Be careful and give my best to your folks. Your mother always took time to chat with me whenever I saw her."

"She does that. I will give them your best." I strode up the street to the station and my car, feeling very confused. I had to admit the attention from Rosemary was flattering, and as much as I hated saying so, Aunt Verbina had a point. The scare this morning at the meeting with the chief brought it all to the forefront.

My mind whirling, I headed back to my apartment to pack a bag and read through the documents the chief had given me. Once back home, I got a cold pop from the icebox and spread all the papers out on the dining room table. The dossiers on Gregor and Ballentine were really just case histories and rap sheets, along with basic information on the crew of the boat and other passengers.

There were also a few pamphlets from Granite Insurance and business cards with "Henry Benson, Insurance Specialist" printed on them, along with a fact sheet on standard insurance terms and background for Henry Benson. A room in the basement of the station downtown held files of fake business cards, passports, company pamphlets, you name it, all printed up and ready to go. If you wanted to be an oil man from Texas, there was a file for it. A hardware store owner? No problem. The phone numbers on all the literature rang to the same answering service downtown. I found it all quite fascinating.

CHAPTER SIX

I checked my pocket watch. Quarter past three. I knew Alan was working the four-to-midnight shift again, and then, lucky him, three days off. On a whim, I decided to head back down to the station and see him. I put the files back together and tucked them in my suitcase, along with the clothes I thought I'd need for the trip and some extra ammunition for my service revolver, just in case.

I tucked in my toiletry kit and the book on astronomy I was reading and latched the lid. I slipped my ticket for the trip into the breast pocket of my suit coat and, with a last look around my apartment, headed toward the door. As I turned the knob, the phone rang. I was tempted to let it ring, but figured it might be the station, so I set my bag down and picked up the receiver.

"Hello?"

"Oh, Heath, I'm glad you're home."

I rolled my eyes and sighed. "Oh, hi, Mom. Actually I was just on the way out. I don't have much time."

"I won't keep you then, dear. I just wanted to tell you I ran into Kristopher Enquist at the market the other day, and he asked about you. You remember Kris."

"Yes, of course. We were friends all through school. How is he?"

"He's doing really well. He's selling cars, you know, and he's married. A real pretty girl—what *was* her name? He told me but I forgot. He showed me a picture, too. She was real pretty."

"Yes, so you said. Good for him."

"Angela or Agatha, or something like that. It will come to me, and I'll call you back."

"You don't have to, Mom, it's fine. If you see him again, tell him hello. I need to run."

"He has a son, too. Four years old already. They named him Thomas Walker Enquist. I remember that because of your friend Tom Walker."

"Yes, we were all friends back then. It's nice they named the child after him."

"Yes, it is. Kris said his wife has a sister who's not married, you know. Did you and Verbina have a talk yet?"

Big eye roll. "Yes, we had tea, we talked. Look, Mom, I really, really need to go. I'm late. I'll call you in the next few days, okay?"

"All right, Heath. Be careful. I'll give Verbina a call later."

"You do that. Say hi to Dad. Bye." I hung up before she could say anything else, picked my bag up, and headed out the door and downstairs to my car, remembering to leave a note for the milkman canceling my order of cottage cheese for the morning.

I found a parking spot on State just before Tenth Street and left my bag in the trunk as I hoofed it to the corner, knowing he took the Number 5 streetcar that stopped on Tenth and State, right by the courthouse. Fortunately this afternoon it was right on time. I smiled as I watched him step down from the streetcar and turn back to help an older woman with a cane clamber down the steps. As she smiled a toothless smile at him, he tipped his uniform cap in her direction and almost ran right into me as he headed to the station.

"Heath! What are you doing here?" He looked startled.

"Hey there, you. I had a few minutes to spare and thought I'd come down and say hello and good-bye."

"Well, gee, nifty. I'm really surprised, but I'm on duty soon."

"I know. But the boat leaves at six tonight, and I wanted to see you in person before I left."

"Boat?"

"Forget I mentioned that. It's classified."

"Forgotten. Look, I'm sorry about getting so upset earlier, Heath, about the weekend and all." He glanced up the block. "But I need to go, or I'll be late."

"I'll walk with you to the station. It's the least I can do, seeing as how I ruined our weekend plans."

Keyes shrugged. "You didn't ruin them, the chief did."

"I should have said no, or at least put up more of an argument."

We started walking, matching our strides. "I won't argue that, but like you said, there will be other weekends, if you want."

"Of course I want. I wanted this weekend, Alan, honestly."

"You didn't have to come all the way down here in this heat just to walk me a couple blocks and tell me that."

"I know, but I wanted to. I was looking forward to spending two nights up north in that fishing cabin with you, just the two of us, I really was."

He nodded. "Yeah, so was I. But duty calls, as you said."

"Yeah, it does."

"I really do understand, Heath."

"Thanks, buddy. I'm glad. You look really great, you know, in your uniform and all."

He laughed. "I look tired. I barely got any sleep last night, and then your call early this morning got me to worrying, and I couldn't get back to sleep."

"Yeah, sorry again about that. But you do look great."

"Thanks, Heath, so do you, but you always do."

We walked past O'Brian's Hardware Store and the market, until we reached the corner.

"Better say good-bye here, Heath."

"Yeah, I suppose so. Not good for us to be seen together too much."

"You took a risk meeting me at the streetcar stop. Spinsky's on with me sometimes."

"You're worth the risk, Alan. And I don't think that old lady suspected a thing."

"Funny, Heath, but the stakes are too high to fool around. You're a detective, remember? You've got your future to think about, your career."

I didn't say anything for a moment. He was so handsome in his uniform, a bead of sweat trickling down his forehead from under his cap. I wanted to reach out and wipe it away.

"I thought you said you understood."

"I do, but I'm still disappointed."

"And you're still sore, too, aren't you?"

"I'll get over it," he said matter-of-factly.

"I didn't mean it when I said you're just a policeman, you know. I was a jerk."

"Yeah, you were. I am getting over it. At least you're a handsome jerk."

"Thanks, Alan. I'll make it up to you, I promise."

"Sure."

I stopped and faced him. "Look, I don't know what is in

my future, okay? Or who, to be honest. Let's take this day by day."

"Day by day. Sure, Heath, play by play. I gotta go, really."

"All right, Alan. I'll give you a call from up there, and I'll see you Sunday night if you want."

"We'll see. Have a safe trip."

We stood there for the briefest of moments, staring at each other. I wanted to embrace him, to kiss him, if only a peck on the cheek, but of course I couldn't. A handshake? Too formal. We finally settled on a slap on the shoulders, and then I watched as he walked away. When I could no longer see him, I headed back to my car, parked on State Street.

I put her in gear and headed down State to Water Street, and from there to the Lake Parkway and south toward Jones Island, an easy drive this time of day. It wasn't the best area, and not someplace you'd want to be alone after dark, but it wasn't the worst, either. I left my Buick in the south lot and grabbed my bag from the trunk. It was a short walk to the dock, though I didn't hurry. It was only four thirty, and the boat didn't leave until six.

The air hung heavy around me, and the heat was oppressive even here along the lakefront. The sky had turned gunmetal gray within the last hour, with dark, rolling clouds moving in from the west. Could be rain, which would cool things off a bit. The flags at the end of the pier hung limp like yesterday's flowers. There was no breeze whatsoever, and nothing much was moving.

I spotted the boat easily enough, moored amongst a couple of tugs and a freighter, about three-quarters of the way down the left side of the pier, facing out toward the lake. She was a long, steam-powered vessel, somewhat squat, with a lone funnel rising from the center like a toothpick in the middle of a hot dog. Probably dating back to the twenties or earlier, she'd definitely seen better days. I approached from the stern and noticed the name painted on the back: the *Speakeasy*. An older, scruffy-looking fellow in a blue jersey was standing above the nameplate, eyeing me.

"Hello," I called out, setting my bag at my feet.

"Ahoy. You must be Mr. Benson. We've been expecting you. Come aboard," the man said in a gruff voice. "I'll meet you at the top of the gangway."

I remembered to slip the wedding ring on my left finger, picked up my bag again, and followed alongside the boat until I reached a narrow gangway. I climbed aboard, clinging to the rope with one hand while managing my suitcase in the other.

"Welcome aboard, Mr. Benson. I'm Willy Gruling, first mate."

"How do you do? How did you know I was Mr. Benson?"

"We have four passengers embarking here in Milwaukee: Benson, Ballentine, Smith, and Slavinsky, and the other three have boarded already. Besides, your bag's got your initials on it."

I glanced down, thankful Henry Benson and I shared the same monogram and irritated for not noticing it myself. "I see. Well, thank you for the welcome. Here's my ticket."

He took it from me and shoved it in one of his pockets without so much as glancing at it, then he extended his hand. As we shook hands, I noticed his were large and callused, and he seemed to be quite strong. The ring finger of his right hand was missing. He was probably in his fifties, though he appeared older. His skin was dark and aged from the sun, his hair bleached, and his dark eyes narrow from years of squinting.

"Let me take your bag. I'll show you to your cabin. You're in number four, one deck below. This is the sundeck. There's an open deck at the stern up here, a smaller area at the bow, and, of course, the wheelhouse, captain's quarters, and funnel in between. The two lifeboats are on either side." He gestured with his large right hand, and I gazed doubtfully at one of the old wooden lifeboats near me, hanging in rather rusty-looking davits. He shrugged at the look on my face. "We ain't failed inspection yet." He picked up my heavy bag effortlessly. "Just this way, Mr. Benson." His rather muscular arms protruded from the cut-off sleeves of the blue jersey, and he had a tattoo of a green mermaid on his hairy left forearm.

He led the way inside down a small set of metal steps to the cabin deck. "The lounge is aft, through that door, the cabins are in the middle through this door, and the dining room and galley in the bow at the end of the passage beyond the cabins. This stair takes you up to the sundeck and down to crew quarters and the hold and engine room. Those areas are off-limits, of course."

"Of course. I think I can remember all that."

"I should hope so. You look like a smart enough fella."

He opened the door on our right, and we took a short walk single file down the narrow companionway to cabin four on the left. Two bunks sat against one of the narrow walls, a sink and a door opposite that, and a wooden swivel chair and desk, both bolted to the floor, on the long wall under the porthole. A faint smell of paint hung in the stale cabin air.

"This is it, all freshly painted just last trip," he said. I glanced about at the pale yellow walls, which complemented the olive green bedspreads on the bunks, embroidered with a large "S."

"Very nice," I said.

"Uh-huh. You can stow your bag under the bottom bunk. If you need to hang anything, there's hooks on the back of the door here. The head's down the way at the end just before the dining room. You share it with the other three cabins."

"Cozy," I stated, not sure of what else to say. It wouldn't have been my accommodation of choice, but it was a short trip and it at least looked clean. I removed my fedora and set it on the desk.

"If you need anything, let us know, Mr. Benson. Our regular steward's out sick, but we've got a new fella by the name of Riker taking his place. He'll be along shortly with towels and such, but he's in the galley at the moment, still figuring things out."

"Very good. Thank you, Mr. Gruling."

"Everyone calls me Willy." He scratched his crotch and adjusted himself.

"All right. Thanks, Willy. It's a bit warm in here, isn't it?"

He shrugged. "A bit. It will cool down once we get out into the lake, though. I wouldn't open your porthole in port because of the flies. They'll eat you alive. They come in swarms like locusts and suddenly the whole room's full of them. The seagulls eat some, but not enough."

"Good to know."

He cocked his thumb. "You got a fan up there in the corner, might help a bit. Anyways, we'll be under way in just over an hour."

"Will there be a lifeboat drill?"

Willy laughed. "This is it. There's a couple of life jackets under the bottom bunk, and there's the two lifeboats up on the sundeck, as you saw. The diagram on the wall tells you all that, too. In case of an emergency, grab a life jacket and head up on deck. Enjoy your trip." He stepped out into the companionway and closed the door.

I switched on the rusty metal fan mounted up in the corner and watched it hum noisily to life. It didn't really do much except stir the air, but that was something. I set my bag on the lower bunk and opened it, removing my toiletries and setting them on the little shelf next to the sink, which had a metal railing around it to keep things in place once the boat was under way. I placed the astronomy book I was reading in the net pocket next to the bunk, and I closed the case and slid it beneath the bed out of sight, wedging it next to the life jackets. I glanced out the closed porthole. I was on the port side of the boat, opposite the pier, and I gazed at the green-brown water lapping lazily at the rust-streaked hull before taking in the tiny room once more. It was a far cry from the *Queen Mary* or *Normandie* indeed, measuring only about seven by nine, but it would have to do. A sharp rap at the door brought me to attention, and I opened it to see a very attractive young man in a crisp white jacket, black slacks, and highly polished shoes, white shirt, and black bow tie, holding a stack of crisply folded white towels.

"Good evening, Mr. Benson. I'm Riker, your steward. I have fresh towels for you."

"Hello, please come in." I stood aside and motioned him in, then closed the door. I felt like we should have a password or something. An awkward silence passed between us as he placed the towels on the bars by the sink and turned to me. "I hope you'll find everything to your satisfaction, Mr. Benson— or Detective Barrington?"

I smiled, relieved. "Yes, yes. I wasn't sure you'd been briefed. You're Grant Riker."

"Best to just call me Riker, sir. And you're Henry Benson, insurance salesman."

"That's right. Is it safe to talk in here?"

"Probably. Slavinsky's in cabin one, opposite and one center from you. Cabin two is next to you. Ballentine and his associate, George Smith, have that one, but they're up in the lounge having a beer. That door next to the sink connects to their cabin, but you can't access it unless they unlock it from their side, too. Still, with your side open, you may be able to hear something."

"Convenient."

"Yes. Cabins two and four connect, and one and three on the other side. My cabin's one deck down, near the hold, and it's even smaller than this, so don't feel so bad. I don't even have a porthole, and I have to share it with the cook."

I laughed. "Tight quarters indeed."

"Cozy can be nice with the right person, but not with that bloke. He's huge," he said, and I swear he had a gleam in his eye. "Best to keep talking to a minimum in here, though, and keep our voices low."

"Of course."

"If you need to talk to me privately, press the call button three times, beep, beep, beep, and I'll come up. Or you can meet me in the hold, if you like. That might be better. Just take the center stairway between the lounge and the cabins. It says Crew Only, but if anyone sees you, feign ignorance. The captain and mate have a cabin up on the sundeck behind the wheelhouse, so no one else goes down to the hold once we're under way except me and the cook."

"Beep, beep, beep. Got it. So Ballentine and his thug are in the lounge, and Gregor Slavinsky's in his cabin?"

"Yes, he got on about twenty minutes ago and went right to his cabin, but he'll probably go up on deck or to the lounge for a drink soon if he hasn't already. I'm serving dinner at eight thirty, once the Chicago people board and we're under way again. The dining room's just forward from here, through the door just past the head, and the galley's in front of that, in the bow. The lounge is aft."

"Yeah, Willy already gave me the lay of the land, more or less."

"He's a character. What do you think of him?"

"He seems on the up-and-up, though I wouldn't want to meet him in a dark alley."

"Nor I. Apparently the guy I'm replacing has been with them two years. They seem like a tight crew."

"What about the captain and the cook?"

"The captain is no-nonsense. Been on the water most of his life. The cook seems kind of simple, but nice enough. He's a big Swede, over six feet tall, all arms and legs, which makes sharing that tiny cabin difficult, to say the least."

I laughed. "Any chance any of them could be involved with Slavinsky or Ballentine?"

"Hard to say, but you'll have to judge for yourself. I've been too busy learning the ropes around here. There's a lot to do. After I finish dinner, I'll be serving cocktails in the lounge. Consider yourself lucky, Detective. You can sit back and relax. Eat, drink, and be merry while I do all the work."

I smiled at him and took him all in. He was shorter than me, about five-nine, with sandy brown hair and green eyes. He was smooth shaven and had a nice smile, cleft chin, slender build, and narrow hips, probably in his mid-twenties.

"Been on the force long, Riker?"

"Six years, though only two out of downtown. I'm hoping to make detective one day. Appreciate it if you can put in a good word for me."

"Well, let's see how well you perform first."

"I think you'll be satisfied with my performance, sir." Was I just imagining that gleam in his eye?

"Time will tell, Riker."

"Yes, sir. Anything I can get you or do for you in the meantime?"

The question was completely innocent and ordinary, but the way he said it made me perk up immediately. It was almost sensual, although very implied.

I shook my head after the briefest pause. "No, thank you, Riker. Maybe later."

He gave me a rather seductive smile, and his eyes sparkled once more. "Very good, sir. Feel free to call me anytime. And don't forget—beep, beep, beep. We have complete privacy in the hold. It's near the engine room, and no one can hear anything once the door is closed. I suspect this is going to be a long weekend with nothing to do but babysit those two."

"You're probably right, but we're getting paid to do it."

"You're getting paid to do it. I'm getting paid to serve dinner, make cocktails, turn down beds, clean the head, wait on everyone, serve breakfast, and be on call in addition to babysitting those two."

"Sounds to me like you won't have much time for anything else."

He grinned slyly. "There's always time, if you make time, Mr. Benson. Once the passengers are in bed, I imagine it will be pretty quiet. The guys tell me you're not married. The ring on your finger goes along with your persona for the trip, I bet."

I looked at him sharply. "What guys?"

"Some of the fellows on the force, guys you used to patrol with."

"You asked about me?"

Riker shrugged. "Your name's come up a few times in passing. The guys like to jabber, you know, sitting in patrol for hours on end. Everyone knows how you nailed those last two murders. You're a rising star, and people talk about rising stars."

"And falling ones," I added, as Aunt Verbina flashed through my mind again.

"I suppose so, not that you need to worry about that."

"I'm a natural born worrier, Riker. So what have they been saying?"

He shrugged. "Nothing special, just how you're not married and don't seem to date, and also how you dress."

"What's wrong with how I dress?"

"Not a thing. But you're always crisp, pressed, and polished. Some of the guys notice, that's all. Sargent Cooley's made a few comments."

"Cooley, that figures." He and I have never seen eye to eye, ever since I didn't show any interest in dating his daughter, Charlotte. "Anything else?"

Riker shrugged. "Oh, I don't know. The guys talk about how you live alone and work a lot. I guess that's how you get ahead, huh?"

"Yeah, something like that. Married to the job."

"Right, but the job's a lousy bedfellow."

"True enough, Riker."

"Anyway, don't let what some of the guys say bother you, Detective. You know how some jerks like to talk."

"I hope you're not one of them."

He grinned again. "Nope, not me. I listen, but I don't say anything, so you don't have to worry there, ever. Anyway, call if you need me, Mr. Benson. I'm at your service." He closed the door behind him as he left.

CHAPTER SEVEN

I went over to the sink and splashed some tepid rust-colored water on my face, his words swirling about in my mind on top of everything else. I used one of the towels to dry off and grabbed my hat off the desk, deciding to go in search of Gregor and the other two, who I figured were in the lounge. The door to the lounge from the stairway was ajar, and I stopped short, listening quietly to the voices within.

"What's with the facial hair, Gregor? Trying to change your image? We used to call you baby face."

"I remember, Benny. I just thought I'd try a beard and mustache for a while, see if I liked it."

I heard Ballentine laugh. "Not helping much. So where is my money, Gregor?"

"It's safe. You'll get it back, Benny. Don't worry."

"I don't worry, Gregor, but George here gets real nervous. When I so generously loaned you the twenty-five grand, you told me you had a can't-lose investment with the K9 Club downtown—booze, broads, and gambling in the back."

"That's right, Benny. It's just taking a little longer to pull together the deal, that's all."

"Sure, sure. I'm a patient man. I recall you even showing me the blueprints and the building, the contract, everything."

"Yeah, down on Second—a great location."

"Right. Only come to find out that building's not even for sale. And now you're on a boat, heading to Michigan by yourself, and you still have my money. Funny, ain't it?"

"But I'm not by myself, Benny. You're here, and so is George."

"Only because we happened to hear you were taking this little trip. You never mentioned it to me."

"You have very good ears."

"I have ears and eyes all over town, Gregor, all over the United States."

"So I've heard."

"Funny," Ballentine said flatly.

"Look, Benny, despite what you heard, the investment is still in the works. The building *is* for sale, but the owner hasn't made it public. He's letting me have first dibs, see? And you'll have a part in the action. You'll be co-owner until I can repay the loan. In the meantime, your money is safe. You'll get every penny back with interest."

"Where is it?"

"Like I said, it's safe, and not telling you where it is keeps *me* safe."

"What, you think I'd hurt you? We're old pals, you and me."

"Right, old pals. So trust me, Benny, okay? You'll get your money back."

"I trust you, Gregor, but you've already missed a payment, and you taking this little trip seems suspicious. If you want to stay safe, not telling me where my money is isn't going to do it."

"I beg to differ, Benny. It's my insurance policy, at least until we get back on dry land."

I listened some more, but they suddenly went silent, so I

pushed the door open and went in. They were glaring at each other from opposite sides of the room, Ballentine and George standing near the port windows and Slavinsky on the starboard side, leaning on the bar. I recognized Ballentine from the mug shot in his file.

He was tall but thick waisted, with short legs. All of his height appeared to be in his torso. His arms were short, too, giving him an odd appearance. He was in his late forties, maybe early fifties, dressed in a well-tailored navy double breasted, a straw porkpie hat on his head. George, on the other hand, was big, solid, and well-proportioned. He had a small, dark mustache, wide-set brown eyes, and a nose that looked like it had been broken more than once. He wore a brown plaid sport coat one size too small and a red bow tie, no hat.

All eyes turned to me as I entered, and I noticed George slip his hand inside his jacket.

"Evening," I said, eyeing them carefully but casually. Slavinsky was a short, thinly built man, not what one would expect of a gangster. He had fine features, pale white skin, and a small mouth, almost lost in a bright red mustache and beard that, I'm sure, he felt made him look tougher. His eyes were small and round beneath thin red eyebrows. He looked like an adolescent boy with facial hair.

"Who are you?" Ballentine growled.

"My name's Benson, Henry Benson. Warm one, isn't it?"

"Too warm for this time of year," Ballentine mumbled, staring at me hard.

"Yes, though it sounds like we're getting under way. That should cool things off a bit." We all listened as the engine throbbed to life a few decks below, grunting and groaning. We could see the green-brown muddy water begin to churn as the propellers started to rotate. I could also see Willy on the dock. A man in a gray pinstriped suit approached and handed him an envelope. Willy tucked it under his arm as he cast off the last of the mooring ropes and leaped effortlessly aboard, the gangway already stowed.

"Yup. Always cooler out on the water," Slavinsky said, his voice quieter and softer than I would have expected.

"And to whom do I have the pleasure?" I asked, still standing in the doorway.

They all looked at each other and then back at me. Ballentine finally spoke.

"Ballentine. Benjamin Ballentine, and this is my associate George. We're in the financial industry, among other things."

"How interesting, Mr. Ballentine. And what about you?" I turned my attention to Slavinsky, who was nervously turning his beer bottle around and around in his hands.

He looked at me suspiciously and then he glanced over at Ballentine and George. "Gregor Slavinsky," he grunted in that soft, low voice. "I'm an investor. Looking at some hotels up in Mackinac."

"I understand it's a good time to invest in properties, Mr. Slavinsky, and of course you want to protect your investments."

"What do you mean by that?"

"Insurance, Mr. Slavinsky. You name it, I cover it." I smiled as I handed him and Ballentine each one of my business cards.

Ballentine took it and handed it off to George, who put it in his wallet. Gregor looked at the one I gave him rather curiously before shoving it in his coat pocket and grunting again. "I don't need any insurance."

I smiled and moved closer to him. "How could anyone not need it, sir? It's protection against fire, flood, earthquake, tornado, hail, wind, and pretty much anything else you can think of."

"I don't think we get many earthquakes in Wisconsin or Michigan, Mr. Benson."

"Have you forgotten we just had one earlier this month?"

He laughed. "That little shake on the sixth? Hardly a quake. My aunt causes more damage when she rumbas."

"We don't insure against rumbas, Mr. Slavinsky, but we certainly cover the rest of it, and isn't it nice to know that you're protected should something happen?"

"I carry my own protection, but thanks anyway."

"If you change your mind, let me know. Life is kismet, Mr. Slavinsky. A turn of the roulette wheel, a roll of the dice, a deal of the deck can change everything in an instant. Why gamble on your possessions and investments?"

"I'll take my chances, Mr. Benson. I've done okay so far. Gotta hit the head, excuse me." He walked away through the door to the cabins.

Ballentine laughed. "Mr. Slavinsky is a bit naïve when it comes to protecting himself, I think, Mr. Benson."

"That is often the case, unfortunately."

"I wouldn't waste your time on him, though. He doesn't have anything of value."

"How unfortunate, but surely his life—"

"That is up for debate. Anyway, he doesn't have any family except for his fat aunt and a sister out in California, and he hasn't seen them in years."

"Oh, my. Well, how about the two of you? Are you both insured?"

"No need to worry about us. George watches over me, I watch over him, and we both watch over Slavinsky."

I raised my eyebrows. "How do you all know each other?"

"We go back a ways, and we've done business together."

"I see. So you're traveling together for business?"

"Not exactly. Mr. Slavinsky has taken out a loan from our institution on a payment plan."

"Oh?"

"When we heard Mr. Slavinsky was taking this little trip, we decided to tag along. We figured a little time away from the city might be nice, isn't that right, George?"

George nodded and took a swig of his beer.

"I believe Mr. Slavinsky mentioned he was going to Michigan to look at properties to invest in."

"That's what he said, yeah."

"Is that what he borrowed the money for?"

"Something like that. You ask a lot of questions, Mr. Benson."

"Just curious."

"Don't be too curious. You know what that did to the cat."

"Meaning?"

"Whatever you want it to mean. George and I are just along to protect our investment. Mr. Slavinsky didn't have much in the way of collateral, and things haven't exactly worked out the way he said they would so far, so we're making sure nothing happens."

"I guess that makes sense."

"Of course it does. You're in the insurance business, Mr. Benson, so you know how important it is to protect one's investments, as you said. I'm just protecting mine."

"Certainly, Mr. Ballentine. That loan must have been rather sizable."

"Sizable enough. A lot of money to him, not so much to me, but I want to make sure I get it back."

"I'm surprised an astute businessman like you would make a large loan like that without sufficient collateral."

"Hey, what did you call him?" George said, setting down his beer bottle and looking at me hard.

"Astute. It means savvy, smart."

"Oh. Right, okay."

Ballentine turned back to me. "Don't mind George, Mr. Benson. He's a little slow, but like I said, he looks after me. And in answer to your statement, I *don't* usually make loans without sufficient collateral, but Mr. Slavinsky and I are old friends. Sometimes one makes exceptions."

"And you're on this boat to make sure you stay old friends."

"Sure, sure. Well, it's been a pleasure, but George and I have a few things to discuss before dinner. Please excuse us as well."

The two of them moved toward the door, steadying themselves against the increasing motion of the boat.

"Of course. I'll see you at dinner if not before."

"By the way," Ballentine said, turning back to me, "what did you say the name of your insurance company was?"

"Granite Insurance."

"Right. Funny, I ain't never heard of it. You don't strike me as an insurance fellow."

"Oh? What do I strike you as?"

"I'm still figuring that out. But remember what I said about curiosity, pussycat."

I felt a shiver run down my spine as I stared at him. "Meow."

"Funny guy. See you at dinner." Ballentine tipped his hat and left the lounge, heading toward the cabins as Slavinsky had.

Chapter Eight

The *Speakeasy* was picking up speed, moving out of the breakwater into the lake before turning south toward Chicago. Riker entered from the starboard door, carrying an envelope.

"A man gave this to Willy just before we pushed off, Mr. Benson. It's addressed to you, from the Granite Insurance Company."

"Thanks."

I opened it and scanned the contents, reading aloud to Riker.

> *Mr. Slavinsky surely has insurance needs. I hope you've arranged for all passengers to be given brochures for automobile, home, life and natural disaster. In Mackinac and everywhere, this trip has to be productive. You haven't booked any new clients recently. A new client would be a coup, and there is always room for more. You will be close to Ontario, Canada, and our sister agency. They have been outselling us, and as you know, Lawrence Marsden outsold you last quarter, and Mr. Brockville outsold you before that. As a reminder, the first four quarters you were with us, you signed two, four, ten and*

eighteen clients respectively. The second year you signed nineteen, twenty-five, twenty-six, and twenty-seven clients. Your third year was even better with thirty-one, thirty-seven, forty-two, and fifty-three. This year your goals are sixty-one, seventy-three, seventy-six, and eighty-four. You missed your first quarter goal by quite a bit, so get cracking!

I studied it for a bit and then handed the letter to Riker, who looked at it with a puzzled expression. "It doesn't make sense. You're not a real insurance agent, and there is no Granite Insurance Company."

"The key is in the quarterly goals," I explained.

"I don't follow."

"The first quarterly goal numbers in the letter are two, four, ten and eighteen, followed by nineteen, twenty-five, twenty-six, and twenty-seven, and so on. If you look at the second, fourth, tenth, and eighteenth words in the note, followed by the nineteenth, twenty-fifth, twenty-sixth, and twenty-seventh, all the way to the eighty-fourth, you get 'Slavinsky has arranged for automobile in Mackinac, and has booked a room Ontario as Lawrence Brockville.'"

He looked at it again. "Oh, yes, I see it now. Code, clever."

"Pretty basic, actually, but it does the job. So it sounds like Slavinsky is definitely planning on slipping across the border once we dock."

Riker handed the letter back to me, and I put it in my breast pocket to burn later.

"But won't Ballentine just follow him?"

"I imagine Slavinsky wasn't counting on Ballentine joining him on this little excursion, and that changes things. Even with Ballentine watching his every move, Slavinsky may still try and make a run for it. Once in Canada, he can get lost in the wilderness, change his identity, and start over. Twenty-five grand would give him a very nice start."

Riker's eyes lit up. "So that would mean he has the money with him."

"Or he's arranged for it to be in Canada, and he can pick it up there."

"Interesting."

"Yes. Get into the cabins when you can and see if you can find anything unusual. Let me know."

"You mean like twenty-five grand?"

"Yes, or a claim ticket, anything. And not just his room, but everyone's."

"Why?"

"Experience has taught me to cover all bases."

"All right. I turn the beds down after dinner, while everyone's in the lounge. I should be able to have a quick look about then."

"Perfect. Keep me posted."

"Will do, Mr. Benson. In the meantime, I guess it's back to work for me."

"No rest for the wicked, they say."

He flashed his beautiful smile at me. "Indeed. But wicked can be fun." He picked up the empty beer bottles and carried them out the door as I admired him from the rear.

My mind was reeling about Slavinsky, Riker, Ballentine, Keyes, and Rosemary, but there wasn't much else to do for now, so I decided to explore. I left the lounge and climbed the metal stairs to the sundeck. I stepped outside and went forward along the narrow deck alongside the funnel, which brought me to the wheelhouse and crew quarters. The door to the wheelhouse was propped open. The man I presumed to be Captain Clark was at the wheel, Willy most likely below decks somewhere, maybe coaxing more power out of the engine.

"Evening. You must be Captain Clark," I said through the open door as I stepped just inside.

He glanced at me sideways. "That's right. Passengers aren't supposed to be in the wheelhouse once we're under way, owner's rules."

"Oh, I'm very sorry."

"It's all right. I'm not the owner, and I won't tell if you won't. Come on in, but don't block the doorway. There's a nice breeze coming in now."

I stepped inside the small wheelhouse, glancing about at equipment, dials, gauges, and machines I knew nothing about but found fascinating. The man at the big brass wheel was the epitome of a captain, or what I thought he should be anyway. He was about sixty years old, with a silvery gray bushy beard and mustache, weathered dark olive skin, and deep-set blue eyes beneath his captain's cap.

"I don't want to bother you, Captain."

"You ain't botherin' me. I know these waters like the back of my hand. I could steer her blindfolded."

"I'd rather you didn't."

He laughed an easy laugh. "Are you a nervous sailor?"

"No, but I don't believe in taking chances."

"Nor I, sir. The captain of the *Titanic*, I'm not. The safety of my boat and passengers is my first concern, always."

"That's reassuring."

"A captain who doesn't think soon finds himself in the drink, and one who takes chances, with the fishes soon dances, I always say."

I smiled. "I'm glad you're at the wheel, then. You seem very conscientious."

"Me and Willy trade off, as it's a long trip. I'll be up here until about ten, then he'll take over for four hours, then I relieve him and take us into Mackinac tomorrow morning at eight."

"It must get rather monotonous."

He shrugged. "It can, but we have things we do to pass the time. Don't worry, though. In all my years, I've never fallen asleep on duty, and neither has Willy, as far as I know."

"I'm sure not, sir."

"So are you Slavinsky, Benson, Ballentine or Smith?"

"Benson, Henry Benson. Insurance sales."

"On holiday?"

"Yes, my wife and kids drove up to the Twin Cities to see her mother, and I'm escaping to Mackinac."

He laughed. "Don't care for the mother-in-law, eh?"

I laughed along with him. "We don't necessarily see eye to eye."

"Nice. I had a wife once, but she left me. Ain't easy being a captain's wife, I suppose. I've got a daughter somewhere, too. Ain't seen her in years."

"I'm sorry."

He spat what appeared to be chewing tobacco into a tin bucket on the other side of him and glanced at me sideways once more. "It's all right. I've got my life, she's got hers. We all do, I guess."

"I guess so. Are you familiar with all your passengers, Captain?"

"Familiar? I know their names and that they paid their ticket. That's all I need to know. The steward does all the pleasantries. We don't have a captain's table on this boat."

"I see. So you don't know Mr. Slavinsky or Mr. Ballentine and Mr. Smith?"

"Should I?"

"No, I just wondered."

"I know them as well as I know you, I guess. In fact, I know you better, seeing as how we've been chatting."

"I suppose you do. Have you been a captain a long time?"

"Too long. I'll probably die out here. I've seen it all. I started out as a cabin boy on the Atlantic when I was fourteen, been on the Great Lakes for over thirty years."

"You must have some great stories."

"Eh, I'm not much of a storyteller. Talk to Willy—he's got some great ones."

"I bet. Did you operate all during the war?"

"Yeah, we kept running, but mostly supplies for the government and ferrying troops from the Great Lakes training center. Did you know there were two aircraft carriers on the lakes during the war?"

"I seem to remember hearing about that, yes. They were worried about submarine attacks against the coastal training facilities."

"Yup, the USS *Sable* and the USS *Wolverine*. They also used them as training ships for naval aviators in carrier landings and takeoffs. Tricky stuff, you know."

"Yes, I can imagine."

He spat again into the tin can, missing this time as the boat crested a wave. "Bet you can't. Was you in the Navy?"

"Uh, no. Medical exemption."

Captain Clark looked at me squarely, then up and down, before turning his attention back to the wheel. "Uh-huh. I was a Navy man during the first war. Tried to enlist in the second, but they said I was too old, so I did what I could here."

I felt embarrassed and ashamed suddenly, though of course I had no reason. I really did have flat feet, and I was exempt from military service because I was a police officer.

"Funny you knowing about the aircraft carriers out here. It wasn't public knowledge unless you were in the Navy or other official capacity on land. I wouldn't think insurance sales would qualify."

"Aircraft carriers on the lake aren't easy to hide, Captain."

"Eh, I suppose not," he muttered, turning to look at me again.

"Well, Captain, I'll leave you be. I understand we'll be in Chicago at seven thirty?"

He fixed his eyes on the water. "Thereabouts. Enjoy your trip, Mr. Benson. Let us know if you need anything."

"Thank you." I stepped out onto the narrow side deck again and felt the wind hit me full force. We were doing approximately ten knots now, and I had to hold on to my hat to keep it from blowing overboard. A glance at my pocket watch told me it was now ten after six, just shy of an hour out of Chicago. The sky to the west was still dark, but it hadn't moved out into the lake yet.

I went to my cabin and got my book, then back to the lounge, but I found reading difficult. The boat was moving about in the depths of the open water, and the motion was affecting me more than I had expected. I gave up and sat staring at the horizon until I realized we were nearing Chicago and slowing down as we approached the dock. It was almost exactly seven thirty by the time the boat had stopped and the ropes were secured. I climbed up to the sundeck to take in the view of the skyline and get some fresh air. The wind had picked up, and the sky north and west was still threatening, but all was calm for now. Once the gangway was in place, Riker climbed down, looking slightly unsure of himself, but sharp in his white uniform jacket.

A door opened in the small building on the pier, and a man and an older, frail-looking woman stepped out. She clung to his arm and took very small steps. They were, I assumed, Mr. Whitaker and his aunt, Mrs. Woodfork, our Chicago passengers. In her free arm, the woman carried a small carpetbag and wore a wide-brimmed dark hat and veil, dark glasses, black gloves, and an old-fashioned long-sleeved black dress that came to her ankles. Around her neck was a cameo choker on a black velvet ribbon. The man, on the other hand, was very stylish, rather short but broad shouldered, sporting a navy blue double-breasted blazer with a white carnation in his lapel, cream slacks, a red tie, and a straw hat with a red band. He had wire-rimmed gold spectacles perched on his nose.

They approached the bottom of the gangway, where Riker waited nervously, shifting his weight from one foot to the other. A porter followed behind the couple, carrying three black cases: two large and one small. When they reached Riker, Mr. Whitaker produced two tickets from his breast pocket, which he handed over. Riker examined them carefully and nodded, his lips moving. He put them in his own pocket and stepped aside, motioning the two of them and the porter to climb the gangway.

That was another lengthy, rather precarious process, as they had to go single file, and they couldn't seem to decide if Mrs. Whitaker, being a lady, should go first or if Mr. Whitaker should go ahead of her to help her up once he reached the top. Finally, Mr. Whitaker led the way, followed by his aunt, and then the porter, who was by now straining under the weight of the bags and sweating beneath his cap.

Riker watched from the dock until all three had made it aboard. He ascended and led the way inside and down to the cabins. A few minutes later, the porter reappeared. Once he was back on the pier, Willy stowed the gangplank, let go the ropes, and leapt back aboard as the engines started up once more, and we were off. I bid the fair city of Chicago *adieu* and headed downstairs to put my book away and get ready for dinner.

I changed my jacket for the evening, transferring the coded letter to the pocket of the fresh one. I searched briefly about for matches to burn it, but finding none, I decided it was safer on my person for the time being. I washed my face and neck and combed my hair, applying a bit more tonic to it and just a small spritz of aftershave to my wrists.

Satisfied, I opened the porthole and turned the cowl, allowing a fresh, cool breeze into the tiny room. The sun had just dipped below the horizon, and the dark clouds that had hugged the lake shore had moved farther out into the lake, bringing with them strong winds. I turned off the fan in the corner, snapped off the light, and headed forward to the dining room, holding on to the side rails in the hall, as the boat had started to rock a fair amount.

CHAPTER NINE

The dining hall was sparsely decorated, painted a pale shade of pink to match the roses in the carpeting. The space was small, narrowing toward the front, with just one table set for six. A small metal rail had been raised all along the edges of the table. Portholes were on both sides of the room, though at this hour it was completely black outside, and on the opposite wall from the entry was a door with a small porthole window leading to what I assumed was the galley.

Since I was clearly the first to arrive, I chose a chair on the port side near the center, which would put me close to wherever Slavinsky and Ballentine sat. The chairs, like the one in my cabin, were bolted to the floor but swiveled to allow people to get in and out. A few minutes later, Riker came in through the galley door, carrying a water pitcher.

"Good evening, Mr. Benson."

"Good evening, Riker. Keeping busy?"

He shot me a foul look. "Nonstop, sir, and more to go. I trust you've been relaxing?"

"Oh yes." I couldn't help but grin, knowing I shouldn't be enjoying this but not being able to stop, either.

"Indeed." He filled my water glass and unfolded my napkin, placing it in my lap a little too attentively, as Mrs.

Woodfork and her nephew entered. She clung unsteadily to his arm. He was now carrying the carpet bag. I stood up until they took their seats at the starboard end of the table. They both looked a bit peaked. A touch of *mal de mer*, perhaps? The potent scent of violets in the room arose from Mrs. Woodfork, who had clearly overdone the perfume, a common malady in the elderly who have lost some of their sense of smell.

"Good evening, I'm Mr. Benson, from Milwaukee. Insurance sales, Granite Insurance Company," I said, taking my seat once more.

"How do you do, Mr. Benson? I'm Alex Bains Whitaker, from Chicago. This is my aunt, Mrs. Woodfork. I'm afraid she's a bit under the weather, and she's saving her voice. I'm hoping this voyage will buoy her spirits as well as sooth her ailments. She's a recent widow, my uncle having passed just six months ago."

"My condolences, madam," I said sincerely.

Mrs. Woodfork glanced in my direction and nodded before looking down at her plate. She was still wearing the outfit she had on when she boarded, clearly a mourning dress, though now I could see her a bit better. She had thick, dark glasses on beneath the veil, too much lipstick, and a prominent beauty mark on her right cheek. Her skin was pale and lined, almost chalk-like.

Her nephew still sported his double-breasted navy jacket and cream slacks, but he now wore a red carnation in his lapel, matching his red tie. I had to wonder where he managed to dig up a fresh carnation in the middle of Lake Michigan. He must have brought it with him.

"A pleasure to meet you both," I said.

"Likewise, I'm sure." I noticed he had placed the carpetbag between his legs.

"I'm sure Riker would stow that bag for you, Mr. Whitaker."

"Hmm? Oh, no thank you. It has my aunt's medicines in it. I like to keep it handy just in case."

"Of course." I sincerely hoped we didn't have a medical emergency on board.

The hall door swung open again, and Gregor Slavinsky entered, unchanged from earlier, except he had left his hat behind and slipped on a rather bright black and white checked sport coat. He chose a chair opposite me.

"Good evening, Mr. Slavinsky."

"Evening, folks."

Before Whitaker and his aunt could reply, Ballentine and his thug came in, taking the seats on either side of Slavinsky.

"Good evening, gentlemen."

"Not so good in my opinion. I don't like all this rocking," Ballentine growled, tucking his napkin in his collar.

"It should calm down by morning, hopefully," I said.

I was impressed by how deftly Riker poured the water, considering the increasing movement of the boat. He placed the pitcher in a round indentation in the sideboard next to the galley door, to keep it from sliding off in rough weather, I assumed. He then disappeared into the galley once more.

"The boat really is moving about, isn't it?" I said, making conversation.

"Yes, I must agree, it's rather rough," Slavinsky replied.

"I'm afraid neither one of us is very good in rough seas, either," Mr. Whitaker said to Slavinsky. "By the way, I'm Alex Baines Whitaker, and this is my aunt, Mrs. Woodfork," he added. "We've already met Mr. Benson here."

"So have we," Ballentine said.

"Ah, splendid, splendid. And who are you three, then?"

"Benjamin Ballentine, with a 'B,' not a 'V,' from Milwaukee."

"A pleasure, sir."

"I'm Gregor Slavinsky, also of Milwaukee. I'm a real estate investor."

"How interesting, Mr. Slavinsky. That leaves you. I didn't catch your name."

George looked at me, then at Ballentine, then finally Whitaker.

"His name's George," Ballentine responded.

"A pleasure to meet you, Mr. George."

"Just George. Everyone calls him George. Isn't that right, George?"

"Yes, sir," George answered, looking somewhat embarrassed.

"Are you a business associate of Mr. Ballentine's, George?"

"George works for me, Mr. Whitaker."

"Oh, I see. Rather like a ventriloquist's dummy, it seems. And what is your business?"

"We're in the financial industry, among other things. George doesn't talk much, so it's best you direct any questions to me."

"Obviously. My aunt here is suffering from laryngitis herself. Perhaps this voyage will help us all."

"You certainly aren't suffering from it, Mr. Whitaker," Gregor said. "Laryngitis, that is."

Whitaker looked offended. "Just trying to make conversation. After all, we're on this trip, all of us together until Sunday afternoon. We might as well be pleasant."

"I agree," I said.

Riker reappeared and everyone looked up at him

expectantly. "Our menu is rather simple tonight: a tossed green salad, roll, and your choice of either chicken or fish, which this evening is a whitefish, fresh from the lake."

"I could use a bourbon," Ballentine stated.

"Red or white wine, coffee, tea, or milk with dinner, Mr. Ballentine. Cocktails are only served in the lounge after dinner. Once the dinner orders are placed, I'll be coming around with beverages."

"I knew I should have brought my own to the table."

Ignoring him, Riker produced a notepad from his left breast pocket and took entrée orders starting with Mrs. Whitaker. Everyone but me and Slavinsky chose the fish. Riker tucked the notepad back into his pocket and disappeared once more into the galley.

"Is this your first trip on the lake, Mr. Ballentine?" I said, taking a sip of my water.

"It is. Hard to believe a lake can have waves like this. I could really use that bourbon to settle my stomach."

"Actually, did you know Lake Michigan is more of an inland sea? It's over three hundred miles long and almost a hundred and twenty miles wide at its widest point. She's over nine hundred feet deep in parts, and hides many shipwrecks." I was pleased I remembered some of the facts from the information sheets the chief had given me.

"Well, aren't you a wealth of knowledge, Mr. Benson? You sound more like a librarian than an insurance salesman."

"Just thought you might be interested, Mr. Ballentine. I'm a bit of an enthusiast when it comes to the Great Lakes."

"Shipwrecks, did you say, Mr. Benson?"

"That's right, Mr. Whitaker. Hundreds of them, I would suppose. Many have never been found, you know. Lake Michigan and all the Great Lakes can wield enormous power."

"I'm afraid that is rather disconcerting, considering what we're currently experiencing," Mr. Whitaker said.

"My apologies. I didn't mean to worry anyone. If I had to guess, I would say we're only in two- to three-foot swells right now. They're not the most comfortable conditions, but there's absolutely nothing to worry about."

"Benson's right. This boat was made to plow through a lot worse than this, I'm sure."

"Thank you, Mr. Slavinsky."

"I still don't like it, though," Slavinsky added.

"Did you say the lake is over nine hundred feet deep?" Ballentine asked me.

"In parts, yes."

"Amazing. No wonder some of those wrecks haven't been found. Anything that went down out here could be lost for good."

"It's entirely possible, but I shouldn't worry. The *Speakeasy* is equipped with two lifeboats and ship-to-shore radio." I remembered the sad-looking boats on the sundeck and shuddered just a bit.

Ballentine laughed. "Good to know. Just don't throw anything overboard that you might want back."

"Wise words, Mr. Ballentine."

"I'm a wise guy."

"I'm sure."

"What's that supposed to mean?"

"I'm just agreeing with you, sir."

Fortunately, Riker appeared at that moment with our meals on a large metal tray he placed on the sideboard. He served each person from there without a single dropped morsel, in spite of having to brace his legs and feet against the rocking and pitching of the boat. The chief made a smart choice in selecting him for this undercover job, though I was starting to feel a bit sorry for him laboring under the heavy trays while I sat back and got waited on. He picked up the tray and went back into the galley, emerging once more pushing a beverage cart, its containers rattling and contents sloshing.

"Wine, coffee, tea, or milk, Mrs. Woodfork?"

"Wine, please," she replied, ever so softly.

"Now, now, dear, the doctor said no alcohol with your medication, remember? My aunt will have milk, please, and I'll have black coffee."

"Yes, sir."

"And you, Mr. Ballentine?"

"Bourbon, straight."

I could tell Riker was resisting the urge to make a smart remark. "Wine, coffee, tea, or milk."

"Wine, then. Red, if those are my only choices."

"But you're having the fish," Riker admonished.

"And I want a glass of red wine with it, you have a problem?"

Riker shook his head. "No, sir, not at all."

"Good. George will have the same."

"As will I. I'm having the chicken."

"Me, too," Gregor added.

"An excellent choice, Mr. Benson and Mr. Slavinsky." He couldn't resist getting in a dig, and he shuddered only slightly pouring the red wine for Ballentine and George.

"I'm not interested in your opinions on my wine choice, Riker, I'm only interested in getting to Mackinac in one piece, safe and sound. I look forward to getting my feet back on solid ground," Ballentine said, cutting into his fish.

"It's always nice to get back to land after being on the water, and vice versa, I've found," I said, taking a bite of my chicken, which was dry. "How is your fish, Mr. Whitaker, Mrs. Woodfork? You must be careful for small bones in whitefish, you know."

Mr. Whitaker looked over at me. "Thank you. The fish is palatable enough. The wine helps. How's the chicken?"

"Sufficient," I replied diplomatically.

"You don't seem to be eating very much, Mrs. Woodfork. Is it not to your liking?"

"She has difficulty swallowing with her throat. Perhaps some broth later."

"I'm sure Riker can arrange that for you. He seems quite capable."

"Yes, quite."

"Are you on holiday, Mr. Whitaker?"

"Yes, I'm taking my aunt to Mackinac for the weekend. She's rather frail, as you can see, and her doctor feels a getaway may do her some good. I'm afraid she took the loss of her husband rather poorly."

"Losing a loved one is never easy, but a getaway does almost everyone some good. You have a kind nephew, Mrs. Whitaker."

She nodded in agreement, her large-brimmed hat rising up and down, casting shadows through the veil onto her pale face. "He's a good boy," she said very softly and rather hoarsely.

"What line of work are you in, Mr. Whitaker?"

"Nothing as interesting as high finance. I run a hardware store in Chicago, family business. This is my first time away in nine years."

"Then it's a well-deserved break, I'm sure."

"I don't mind the hours or the work, most days. I enjoy what I do. I'm a widower with no children, so what else do I have? My aunt has been like a mother to me, however, and when the doctor said a change would do her good, I made the arrangements."

"I have an aunt I hold rather dear myself. I hope you both return well rested and healthy," I said.

"Very kind of you. Have you been in the insurance business long, Mr. Benson?"

"Five years. It has its ups and downs."

"Everything does, including this boat," Mr. Whitaker replied.

That caused general laughter all around, including from me.

"And you, Mr. Ballentine?" I said, turning my attention once more to the gangster across from me. "You said you are in the financial industry."

"That's right. Investments, loans, mortgages, that sort of thing. I take care of people's needs. I also own several businesses. I'm a bit of an entrepreneur."

"How interesting. Have you been doing that long?"

"Long enough. I believe I told you earlier that I've got a loan out right now, a fairly tidy sum that I'm keeping an eye on. I don't want to let it slip away."

Slavinsky shifted uncomfortably in his seat and stabbed at his chicken.

"How would a loan slip away, Mr. Ballentine?"

"It can happen, Mr. Benson. Someone gets behind on their payments, they get in over their head, and suddenly the loan is in default and I'm out my money. I'm not about to let that happen. There's also some people who attempt to take the money fraudulently."

"How very interesting," I said.

"Yes, though they rarely get away with it. They make false claims, then try to take the money and run. It doesn't go so well for them in the end."

I glanced over at Slavinsky, who was looking rather pale.

"Well, I certainly hope all goes well for you, Mr. Ballentine."

"I have no doubt I will be successful, Mr. Benson." Ballentine tossed his napkin onto his plate. "I'm finished. This damned boat is moving too much for my liking."

"No dessert? I heard it's cherry pie tonight," I said, finishing up my chicken.

"Not for me. You all go ahead. I'm going to the lounge for a real drink. Come on, George."

George took a last bite of his fish and dropped his napkin on his plate as he got to his feet to follow Ballentine out.

"Well, that was rather rude," Whitaker said after they'd left.

"Not surprising, I assure you. Mr. Ballentine doesn't stand on manners," Gregor said, still looking pale.

"Clearly."

The rest of us finished our meals, including dessert, except for Mrs. Woodfork, who just sat there looking peaked and uncomfortable. Every once in a while, she would raise her veil to take a sip of milk or some water, but that was about it. Her hand trembled unsteadily with the rigors of old age, and I noticed she still wore her black gloves.

When everyone was finished, her nephew helped her slowly to her feet, and Gregor and I followed suit.

"Shall we all join Mr. Ballentine and George in the lounge?" I asked.

"I'm afraid my aunt is tired, Mr. Benson. I think we'll just retire." Using his left hand to steady her, he reached down with his right and picked up the carpetbag.

"But I don't think Riker has had time to turn down your beds yet," I said, knowing Riker would want to look around their cabin.

"Oh. Well, if he can do ours first, that would be appreciated."

As if on cue, Riker appeared once more from the galley.

"Mrs. Woodfork and Mr. Whitaker would like to retire, Riker. Would you mind terribly making up their room right away?"

"Not at all, sir. I'll just take the dishes to the galley and then be there straight away."

"Splendid, thank you. We'll see you in the lounge, then, when you're done."

"Yes, sir."

CHAPTER TEN

The four of us made our way down the cabin passage, past the stairs and into the lounge, where Ballentine sat enjoying a bourbon straight. George was holding what appeared to be a beer. Both of them were smoking.

"I didn't know it was an open bar, Mr. Ballentine. Isn't Riker supposed to be serving us?"

"He's got enough to do, and I've been waiting long enough, Benson, so I helped myself. Can't find any goddamned ice, though."

"There is a lady present," I reminded him.

Ballentine glanced at Mrs. Woodfork, who had taken a seat next to the door. "My apologies, madam."

She nodded her head ever so slightly. Whitaker put the carpetbag by her feet and started pacing back and forth somewhat unsteadily, balancing himself against the movement of the boat. I positioned myself near Ballentine, and George and took a seat, observing. Gregor stood by the bar, apparently trying to decide if he should follow Ballentine's lead or wait for Riker. Finally, he lit a cigarette. "Care for a smoke, Mr. Whitaker?"

Whitaker turned toward Slavinsky and braced himself

against a table. "A capital idea, Mr. Slavinsky, but I'll have one of my French rolled cigars. They're all I smoke, very smooth, you know," he replied. Whitaker took out a silver cigar case and lit up, careful to blow the smoke away from his aunt. "Anyone want to try one?"

"I'll stick to cigarettes, thanks." Slavinsky turned his back to the room and leaned on the bar.

"I don't smoke, Mr. Whitaker," I answered.

"Give me a good Cuban cigar if I'm going to smoke them," Ballentine said. "I like my cigarettes plain and simple, like George here." He laughed at that, but no one else did. George took a drag on his and looked uncomfortable.

"Suit yourselves." Whitaker managed a few impressive smoke rings before continuing his unsteady pacing back and forth across the small room. Mrs. Woodfork held her handkerchief to her nose.

"You seem rather agitated, Mr. Whitaker. Is the motion bothering you?"

"Hmmm? What? No, it's fine. I'm getting used to it, I suppose."

"Why don't you sit down and relax before you fall over? Riker shouldn't be too much longer."

He paced a few more steps, took a seat next to his aunt, then almost immediately got back up again, apparently unable to sit still. "I could use a whiskey, straight."

"I saw a bottle behind the bar, Whitaker," Ballentine volunteered.

"Thanks." He stepped behind, poured himself a generous drink, then continued to pace and smoke.

"Any better?" I asked.

He glowered at me. "It settles my nerves. I just want this whole trip to be done with, to be back on dry land. I doubt I will sleep well tonight, though this will help."

"Hopefully Mrs. Woodfork will manage to get some rest," I said.

He almost laughed. "She has a sedative. I might imbibe myself tonight." He drained the glass and set it on the bar just as Riker appeared.

"Your room is ready, Mrs. Woodfork, Mr. Whitaker."

"Fine, fine. We bid you all good night, then, at least as good as it's going to get." He picked up the carpetbag once more, extinguished his cigar, and held out his arm for his aunt, who dutifully took it and rose to her feet. The rest of us followed suit as the two of them made their way out the door, he holding the carpet bag, she leaving a scent of violets behind her.

When they had gone, Ballentine turned to the bar and growled at Riker, "About time you showed up. Another bourbon, and where's the goddamned ice?"

"Coming right up, Mr. Ballentine." Riker stepped behind the bar and opened a cabinet, then lifted a latch that revealed a cooler. He scooped ice cubes into a glass followed by three fingers of bourbon, and he handed it over to Ballentine, who took it without thanks as he handed his empty glass back to Riker.

"Anything for you, Mr. Slavinsky? Mr. Benson?"

"A vodka martini, dry, two olives," Gregor said. "I don't do bourbon or whiskey. Too much of the bad stuff during Prohibition put me off them."

Riker mixed his cocktail and handed it over.

"I'll take a ginger ale, Riker, no ice."

"Yes, sir." Riker poured my drink, then wiped down the bar surface with a rag from below. "If you will all excuse me, I need to finish the other cabins. I'll be back shortly."

"Poor guy. They work him like a dog," Slavinsky muttered, putting out his cigarette and lighting another.

"Some people, Mr. Slavinsky, work for a living. You might try it sometime," Ballentine said sarcastically.

Gregor turned his back again, ignoring him, and took a sip of his martini.

"I do feel a bit sorry for Riker," I added sincerely. "He has a lot to do."

"I'll be sure and tip him well when we get off this tug," Ballentine said. "You all do the same. I hope you can come up with the money to do that, Slavinsky. Your own money, that is."

"I'll manage, Benny," he said, his back still turned.

"Benny?"

"Huh? Oh, that's a name Mr. Slavinsky used to call me. I go by Benjamin or Mr. Ballentine now."

"I see."

He glowered at Slavinsky's back. "Let's stick to Mr. Ballentine, Slavinsky. It's more professional. We're not kids anymore."

"Whatever you say, Mr. Ballentine."

"I like that answer. Shows intelligence, which you seem to be lacking lately."

Gregor drained his martini. "The alcohol must be eating my little gray cells." He set his glass on the bar and turned to face us. "Anyway, it's been a long day, and I'm done in. I think I'll go to bed as well."

"Good timing, I'd say. Here comes Riker. He must be finished with the rest of the cabins."

"Everything all right, gentlemen? Anyone need anything?" Riker stepped back behind the bar.

"No thanks. I was just saying I'm going to bed." He slid his empty glass toward Riker, put out his cigarette, and turned to me. "By the way, Mr. Benson, if you're looking for insurance customers, you may want to look up my sister, Vondell Strobel.

She's a widow with four kids, lives in California." Slavinsky took out the business card I had given him earlier and wrote down his sister's name and address, then handed it back to me. "Get in touch with her when you get back to town."

"Sounds like an excellent candidate, Mr. Slavinsky, but I'm afraid I don't cover California."

"Too bad. I try to send her money when I can, but you know how it goes. Hang on to her contact information anyway, will you? Maybe you can pass it along to someone."

"Of course."

"Thanks. Well, good night, gentlemen. I'll see you at breakfast."

"Sleep well, Mr. Slavinsky," I said.

Ballentine and George grunted in his general direction.

I wasn't sure what to do next. Slavinsky had gone to his cabin, but Ballentine and George were here, as was Riker. I decided I should at least check on Slavinsky, knowing Riker could watch the other two. I finished my ginger ale and handed the glass to Riker. I then excused myself on the pretense of going to the head. Down the corridor, I stopped at the door to Slavinsky's cabin and listened. I could hear him milling about inside, presumably getting ready for bed. I checked my watch—quarter to ten. It had been a long day for me too, and I stifled a yawn.

I let myself into my cabin. Riker had been there to turn down the bed and put out fresh towels. I wondered if he'd had a look around at my personal things, too, though nothing looked disturbed. I was tired, but a little cool water to my face and neck helped, and I loosened my tie and collar before heading out again. I used the head, then walked back to the lounge just a few minutes past ten. George sat alone, staring out the window into the blackness and smoking yet another cigarette. Riker was putting things away and tidying up. The general lights were off, but a soft pink glow came from a table lamp next to George's chair.

"What happened to Mr. Ballentine?"

"The bar closes at ten, so Mr. Ballentine asked me for a bucket of ice and went to his cabin. I'm just cleaning up, waiting on you and George."

"I see."

George gazed up at me. "The boss has a bottle in the cabin. He wanted to be alone for a while, so I figured I'd wait here."

I pictured Ballentine in his cabin, bourbon in one hand and something else in the other. "Do you mind if we stay in here for a bit, Riker?"

He shrugged. "Fine with me."

"Thanks." I walked over to the bar and leaned in close to him, speaking softly. "Meet me in my cabin in an hour."

He nodded, an odd expression on his face, almost a smirk. I dismissed it and sat down next to George as Riker turned out the last bar lights.

"Good night, gentlemen."

"Good night, Riker. Thanks."

When Riker left, I turned back to George. "Enjoy your dinner, George?"

He looked up at me from a cloud of smoke. "I've had better."

"As have I, but it sufficed."

"Yeah, I suppose so. This ain't the *Queen Mary*."

"Nor the *Île de France*. Funny, I made that same comparison earlier today."

He laughed. "The beer helped, but the boss won't let me have more than one or two, and the bar's closed now, anyway."

"Too bad. Mind if I join you?"

"Looks like you already have."

Now it was my turn to laugh. "True. Is that all right?"

"Fine by me." He stubbed out his cigarette and offered me one from his gold case. "Cigarette?"

"Thanks, no, I don't smoke."

"That's right," he said, taking one. "You mentioned that earlier. To each their own."

"Impressive cigarette case you have there."

"Thanks. The boss gave it to me for Christmas last year, engraved and everything."

"That was nice of him."

"Yeah. He can be generous. I gave him a tie and a poem I wrote."

"You write poetry?"

"Sometimes. It relaxes me. You think that's queer?" He looked somewhat embarrassed.

"Not at all, George. I think it's marvelous. Not everyone can do that."

"Mr. Ballentine didn't seem to think much of it. I don't think he liked the tie, neither. He's never worn it."

"Maybe he's saving it for a special occasion."

"Yeah, maybe," he said, but he looked doubtful.

"You don't seem like the poetry-writing type, if you don't mind my saying so."

"Most people think I don't do much, don't know how to do much."

"Everyone has hidden talents and abilities, George. I guess I shouldn't assume things, shouldn't judge you on appearances."

"Why should you be any different?"

"I like to think I'm different. I try to be at least. I'd love a handwritten poem. It's very personal and a wonderful gift."

He shrugged and grunted something incoherent.

"So Mr. Ballentine wanted to be alone tonight?" I said, changing the subject.

"Yup, for a while. He likes to read his pin-up magazine in private before bed."

"Oh, I see. And what if you had wanted to go to sleep?"

He blew a cloud of smoke into the already very smoky air. "Wouldn't have mattered. He's the boss. I don't want to go to sleep just yet, anyway. I'm not tired."

"I'm surprised Mr. Ballentine didn't book adjoining cabins for you two so you each could have some privacy."

He shrugged. "Mr. B likes to keep me close. I'm his bodyguard, among other things. I stay in a room next to his back home, but I think the boss thought these cabins would be larger. He asked for adjoining cabins when he saw them, but they was filled up."

"Yes, apparently I got the last one. Sorry about that."

"It's all right. It's a short trip."

"Are you having trouble with the motion, George?"

He shrugged again. "Doesn't bother me much. I just wasn't ready to sleep, so I stayed in here and let the boss be. I usually give him a half hour or so."

"I hope I'm not intruding."

He looked at me rather dully. "Nope. I'm just sitting here, same as you."

"Have you worked for Mr. Ballentine long?"

He blew out another breath of smoke, then inhaled again before answering. "Long enough. Too long, maybe, I don't know. It's all I know, though—working for him, I mean. We were pals in school, I took care of him, he took care of me, and it's still that way. Probably always will be, I guess."

"Mutual satisfaction."

"Yeah, I guess. I never got to finish school—dropped out in eighth grade. The teachers and me didn't get along."

"I see. What would you do if you didn't work for him?"

"If I didn't work for Mr. Ballentine?" He looked at me deeply. "No one's ever asked me that before, Mr. Benson."

"Well, I'm asking."

"You're a funny guy. Most people don't talk to me at all. I stand in the shadows while they talk to him."

"But he's not here right now."

George glanced about the lounge, as if making sure. "No, he's not."

"Why don't people talk to you?"

"I don't know. I guess most people think I'm stupid."

"Do they?"

"Yeah, it's because of my size, I guess. Do I look stupid to you?"

"Not at all."

"Mr. Whitaker called me a ventriloquist's dummy at dinner earlier."

"That's not entirely accurate, George. I think what he meant was Mr. Ballentine treated you like one because Whitaker would ask you a question, and Ballentine answered for you."

"He does that a lot."

"And you don't like it."

He shrugged. "He's my boss. I do what he says, and he can do what he wants."

"But you're not stupid."

"He thinks I am. Plain and simple, I believe he said earlier, like his cigarettes."

"Then he's wrong. You have kindness, depth, and intelligence in your eyes. I can see that."

He looked surprised. "Can you? Really? Most people can't. Even my own mum called me stupid, but I'm not."

"No, you're not. There's a difference between education and intelligence, you know."

"That's funny."

"Why?"

"I dunno, just sounds funny. I guess it makes sense, though. You don't have to be educated to be intelligent, is that what you're saying?"

"That's exactly what I'm saying, George. An intelligent man can be educated if he wants to be. A stupid person cannot."

"Huh. I write my poetry a little, like I said before, and I play the piano—mostly self-taught—and I sing, too. And I'm real good at math."

"That's wonderful. I've always wanted to play the piano, and I'm terrible at math."

"I'm sure you have your own strengths, Mr. Benson. Everyone does, like you said before."

"Thanks. What are your boss's strengths?"

"Oh, he's all right. He knows his stuff, he gets things done. He knows all kinds of people and how to talk to them. He's clever."

"Sly like a fox."

"Yeah. Intelligent and educated."

"He seemed to be watching Mr. Slavinsky a lot during dinner," I said.

"Was he? I hadn't noticed." He stubbed out his cigarette and lit up another, his case almost empty.

"My observation, anyway. Mr. Ballentine mentioned Mr. Slavinsky had borrowed a large sum of money from him on a payment plan."

"You're a funny man, Mr. Benson. You ask a lot of questions, just like the boss said."

"Just in my nature, I suppose. I'm a curious fellow."

"A curious cat. You really are different, and you're out here on this boat all by yourself."

"My wife and kids are in Minnesota, visiting her mother."

"You shoulda went with."

"I was supposed to, but we had a bit of an argument."

"That's too bad, Mr. B. Have you been married long?"

"No, just a few years. We're still getting to know each other." I took the photograph the chief had given me out of my wallet and handed it to him.

"Nice-looking dame—lady, I mean. Kids are cute, too."

"Thanks. That's Janie and Alex. Ellen's my wife."

"I had a girl once, but it didn't work out. The boss, he keeps me busy, keeps me moving," George said, still staring at the photograph in his hand.

"Don't you ever get lonely, George?"

"Sure I do. I ain't a monster. I'm just a guy, like you." He handed the photograph back to me, and I returned it to my wallet.

"Of course you are. I get lonely, too. Especially at night when I'm all alone with my thoughts and the stars. I was just wishing I could call Alan right now."

"Alan?"

"Ellen, my wife," I corrected myself quickly.

"Oh. It sounded like you said Alan."

I felt my face flush and was glad of the darkened room. "It's all right. Alan and Ellen sound a lot alike."

"Yeah, I suppose. My girl's name was Edith," George said softly, stroking his mustache.

"That's a pretty name."

"Yeah."

I turned my head and looked out the window into the blackness. "I'd like to hear Ellen's voice right now, George. We had a stupid argument right before I left. Sometimes I miss her so much, and then other times I wonder if I'm not rushing into things, settling down too quickly. I was single a long time. It's funny. Until I met her, I didn't feel lonely nearly as often as I do now when we're apart."

"Because you didn't know what you were missing."

"Yeah, I guess so. But there are many others just as attractive, as appealing, tempting me."

"Temptation is powerful, Mr. B. But the way I look at it, if you've got someone already that feels about you the way you feel about them, that is worth a lot. Why go looking for silver if you've already found gold?"

I smiled. "You're definitely not stupid, George. In fact, I'd say you're a smart cookie."

He grinned, and I noticed he was missing a couple of teeth. "Thanks, Mr. B." He pulled out a gold watch from his vest pocket and stared at it before putting it away again. "Well, I'd better get off to bed myself. Long, early day tomorrow, and I imagine the boss is all finished by now."

"Right. Well, thanks for the company."

"Sure thing." He got to his feet, smoothing out the crease in his pants. "Oh, and Mr. Benson?"

"Yes?"

"You could still learn to play the piano if you really wanted to."

I nodded through the haze of smoke. "You're right. And you could still do something besides work for Mr. Ballentine, George. I mean, if you wanted to."

"Yeah? And what would I do? Sell insurance?"

"I bet you'd make a great math teacher or music teacher. Maybe even a cabaret singer or piano player."

He laughed. "Sure, come by the Painted Pony and drop two bits in my tip jar at the piano."

"Just something to think about, George."

"Yeah, I know. Thanks. And make that call once we get to shore again. To Ellen."

I watched him as he walked to the door, the cigarette dangling from his lips.

"No smoking outside of the lounge, remember."

"Oh yeah, right." He walked over and ground the cigarette out in the ashtray. "Have a good night, Mr. Benson. You're a nice man. Don't ask too many questions, though, okay? The boss don't like it none."

"I'll try not to. And thanks, George. Keep writing that poetry."

He nodded and gave me a small, rather sad smile, then he slipped out, closing the door behind him. I turned the last light out in the lounge and made my way down the passage to cabin four, unlocked it, and slipped inside.

CHAPTER ELEVEN

I had almost forgotten I'd arranged to meet up with Riker to find out if he'd discovered anything I should know about in the cabins. I took the coded letter from my coat pocket and set it on the desk, knowing I should burn it, but I still didn't have a match. I'd have to ask Riker for one. I slipped my coat off and waited nervously. I checked my reflection in the small mirror over the sink at least three times, smoothing out my hair and adjusting my tie. Finally I slipped the shoulder harness off and tucked it into my suitcase beneath the bottom bunk for safekeeping.

This is strictly business, I kept telling myself, and yet the spark between us both worried and excited me.

I jumped a bit as a sharp rap came at last at the cabin door. Riker, in all his handsome glory, held a silver tray with a white tea service, cup and saucer on it, all emblazoned with the letter "S" in red.

"Your tea, Mr. Benson."

I looked at him blankly for a few seconds before I realized the tea was a cover in case anyone saw him coming into my cabin.

"Ah, yes. Thank you, Riker. Please set it on the desk." I stepped aside to allow him in, then closed and locked the door behind him. I watched, admiring the view as he set the tray on the table next to the coded letter and raised the edges of the desk to keep the tray from sliding off. I realized too late he could see me in the mirror admiring his posterior.

He turned and smiled at me, "My pleasure, sir. Anything else I can do for you?"

I lowered my voice, still looking at him. "Find anything of interest in the cabins when you did the turndown?"

He shrugged, unbuttoned his jacket and flopped on the bottom bunk, making himself a little too comfortable. "Oh, that. Not really. I didn't have enough time for a really thorough search, but I guess I did all right. Gregor Slavinsky is very tidy, though not as tidy as you." He laughed, glancing about.

"I like things a certain way."

"So I noticed. The big thing I found in his cabin was a hotel reservation for some place called Moose Head Lodge in Sault St. Marie, Ontario, under the name Lawrence Brockville, and a confirmation letter for an automobile to meet the boat at the dock in Mackinac."

I whistled. "Just like the police said. I'd love to know where they get their information."

Riker nodded. "He's definitely planning a run for the border once we dock."

"Yes. The big question is what we do about it, if anything, and what will Ballentine do if he finds out."

"We'll have to wait and see."

"Yes. I think I should plan to be first off the boat so I can observe and follow if necessary. Did you find anything else?"

"Not much else. Clothes, shoes, luggage, toiletries, and a book on the Great Lakes, with the section on Lake Michigan dog-eared. It looks like he was charting our course as we went along. I flipped through the rest of it to see if anything was hidden in the pages, but no dice. Oh, and I found a bottle of whiskey in one of the drawers."

"Interesting. He mentioned earlier he doesn't like whiskey, and he was having a martini before. What about our friends next door?"

"Pretty much the same thing, though not nearly anywhere near what I'd call tidy. Things were strewn about all over the place. Of course, it's a small space for two fellows to be sharing."

"These cabins are small for even one person," I said.

"Again, you should see mine." He grinned at me, and I noticed he draped his left hand rather casually on his crotch, his left leg on the floor, his right leg up on the bunk.

"Watch your shoes on the bed, Riker."

"Right, sorry." He slipped his shoes off and dropped them on the floor, and then he took his jacket off and put it unfolded on top of his shoes. "Ah, that feels much better, anyway. I've been on my feet all day, and those shoes are murder. That jacket is a bit tight, too. You should make yourself comfortable. It's getting late, you know." He undid his shirt collar and propped the pillow beneath his head.

Damn, he was attractive and enticing. I slipped my own shoes off and tucked them under the bunk, unavoidably brushing against his leg. He didn't move.

"Loosen your tie, or take it off. It's just the two of us."

I undid the knot and slipped off the tie, folding it carefully before setting it in one of the desk drawers next to my clean socks and underwear.

Riker laughed. "You really are something."

"What do you mean?"

"I was in the Navy during the war. We had to keep things tidy in the barracks, but I've never seen a civilian so clean and organized."

I felt my face flush a bit. "I like things a certain way, that's all."

"Hey, don't get angry. It's fine, really. I wish I could be more like you."

I wondered how much like me he really was. I undid the cufflinks of my shirt and dropped them into the drawer and rolled up my sleeves.

"Better?"

"Yes," I said.

"Good."

I sat in the swivel desk chair and turned it to face him as he lounged on my bed. "So besides a mess, did you find anything else of interest in Ballentine and George's cabin?"

"Nope. A case of bullets, a copy of the latest racing form, a half-empty bottle of bourbon, a wad of used chewing tobacco in their sink, a half-eaten candy bar, and a framed photo of some old dame in pearls—probably one of their mothers."

"Probably George's," I said.

"Could be. She kind of looked like him, mustache and all."

I laughed. "No copy of the *Financial Times*?"

"Not hardly. The only reading material in their room I could find was a cheesecake magazine. It certainly was well worn, and some of the pages were stuck together. Apparently, at least one of them likes brunettes in high heels, stockings, and garters."

"That would be Ballentine, from what George mentioned earlier."

"I kind of figured that."

"What about Mr. Whitaker and his aunt?"

Riker had begun running his fingers along the fly of his trousers as he spoke. "Nothing much in their cabin to speak of besides the usual stuff you'd expect. Again, tight quarters, and always more difficult when a woman is involved. It looks like Mrs. Woodfork has commandeered the desk for her dressing table, with bottles, potions, creams, lipsticks, powders, and everything all over the place. She must buy that violet perfume by the quart. There were two big bottles of it. For an old lady, she certainly packs a lot of girl stuff. Her makeup case is quite extensive."

"Funny. The makeup is probably an attempt to cling to her lost youth."

"A failed attempt, I'd say. Whitaker has the top bunk—I found some of his French rolled cigars in the netting up there. And it looks like he has just one drawer for all his things. But again, nothing unusual in their cabin: clothes, toiletries, shoes, a book on Greek tragedies, a couple of women's fashion magazines."

"Mrs. Woodfork reads women's fashion magazines?"

"I don't think they belong to Whittaker." He chuckled lightly, looking up at me. He had undone his tie along with several buttons of his shirt. "She has all the current fashion magazines, but I'm not sure why. Her clothes are all about twenty-five years out of date."

"Yes. She's in mourning, of course, but her attire is still very out of date." I shook my head. "How do you remember so much in such detail? You couldn't have been in each room for more than a few minutes."

Riker smiled broadly. "I have a photographic memory. It's one of the reasons the chief thinks I may make a good detective one day."

"I should say so. A photographic memory comes in handy in this business."

"Either that or cheating at cards."

I laughed. "I think you're making the right career choice. You're a man of many talents."

"You have yet to find out." Riker grinned seductively at me.

I blushed, ignoring his comment. "So, does your memory recall anything else?"

"Well, Mr. Whitaker must have trouble sleeping, because he has a bottle of phenobarbital in his suitcase."

"That's a barbiturate."

"Yes, widely used for insomnia. My uncle used to take it."

"Interesting," I said. "He had mentioned a sedative earlier for his aunt. Perhaps that's what he meant. I wonder what's in that old carpetbag."

"The one with his aunt's medicine in it?"

"Yes. A rather large bag for medicine."

"From the looks of her, she needs a rather large bag of medicine, poor dear. Whitaker must be devoted to her. I found an eight-by-ten glossy headshot of the old lady in his suitcase, too."

"She probably gave it to him as a gift. Old ladies think people like that. Did she sign it, too?"

"No, I didn't see any signature, and it wasn't even in a frame. Just the headshot."

"Hmph. So that's the lot of them, then."

"Yup. Not anything exciting—no rogue guns, no poisons, no stash of twenty-five grand—at least none that I could find— no claim tickets to a train station luggage room in Canada. It's pretty much what I expected. So, it looks like we'll have a nice, quiet trip until we dock, and I think we should make ourselves comfortable."

"But once we dock in the morning, all hell could break loose if Slavinsky decides to go through with his plan for a run to the border. We have to be prepared for anything. I assume you have a gun?"

"Yes, of course. It's locked in my bag right now. This damned uniform is too tight to wear it underneath."

"Hopefully, you won't need it, but we need to be prepared.

If Gregor runs and Ballentine follows, there could be a shootout. I think it would be best if I'm off first, then Gregor, and Ballentine and George. Try to keep Mrs. Woodfork and Mr. Whitaker on board for a while where they'll be safe."

"I'll see what I can do, and I'll be ready. But the morning is hours away, you know. We can't do anything right now. The motion of the boat makes some people queasy, but I find it useful for some things." He grinned at me then, and I felt my face flush once more, like a schoolboy. "By the way," he continued, "I don't know if you noticed, but I brought some lard up from the galley. It's on the tray next to the tea, under the cover."

I glanced over at the tray, sliding about a bit on top of the desk. "What for?"

"Come on, Heath. You don't mind if I call you Heath, do you?"

"I suppose not, though my cover name is Henry."

"Henry, then. Surely you've been around the block a time or two, at least from what I've heard."

"Where did you hear that?" I asked, bristling.

"Does it matter?"

"It does to me. The same fellows you mentioned earlier?"

"Just around. What's the big deal? I'm discreet, and I know you are."

"You're also very forward and assuming, Riker."

"You asked me to your cabin tonight, remember?"

"To find out what you uncovered in the cabins after dinner."

He laughed lightly. "And that couldn't wait until morning? You know that if I had found anything important, I would have reported it to you right away. It was just you, me, and George in the lounge."

"But George could have overheard."

"We could have gone on deck for a few minutes under some pretense and talked privately there."

I felt my face flush, and I had to admit to myself he was right.

He lay on his side now, watching me, still rubbing himself. "Life's short, and so is the night, Henry. We have to take the chances as they come."

"Have you had many chances?" I asked him, not making eye contact.

He laughed again. "Lots in the Navy. Five or six of us got together regular. Ernie was the best, until they shipped him overseas. We were all stationed here at the Great Lakes center."

"I was exempt from service—flat feet and policeman."

"Too bad. You missed a lot of fun."

"It sounds like it. What about after you got out?"

"I thought about being a Navy career guy, but I couldn't take all the rules and whatnot. You probably would have fit right in. They like neat, tidy guys."

"I wanted to serve, I just couldn't."

"I understand, buddy, really. Anyway, I became a policeman after I was discharged. That was right after I met Mary Jane."

"Who's Mary Jane?"

"My wife."

I stood up quickly and almost fell over, the movement of the boat throwing my balance off. "Your wife?" I called out, too loudly I realized as I clutched the edge of the desk for support.

"Yeah, didn't I mention her?"

"You most certainly did not. And you're not wearing a ring," I said, watching him running his left hand up and down his crotch, beneath which something large had formed in his pants.

"She wears the ring, not me. We're old-fashioned like that."

"Oh yes, very old-fashioned," I said sarcastically.

"Sit down before you fall over, Henry."

"I just didn't expect you to be married. I mean, with everything you've said, everything you've done." I sat down carefully, turning the seat once more to face him.

"A man can be married and still have his buddies, Henry."

My Sunt Verbina's face and words flashed through my mind once more.

"Aren't you worried she'll find out?"

"Find out what? Who's going to say anything? Like I said, I'm discreet. Even if someone did say something, she wouldn't believe it. She's too busy taking care of the baby to pay any attention to much else anyway, including me lately."

"Baby?"

"Geez, Henry, yeah. That happens when two people get married, you know? We have a little girl, Jane Marie, after Mary Jane, get it?"

"Yeah, yeah, I get it." I nodded, my head swimming.

"Look, Mary Jane's a sweetheart, a great gal, and I love her to pieces, okay? But there's nothing wrong with having some buddies, too. I mean, some guys have fishing buddies, some have golf buddies, I have, well, another type."

"I can't believe this."

"I know several guys right in town, even a couple on the force, that are married but like their men friends, too."

"Who?"

He laughed. "I don't kiss and tell. I don't name names for no one or nothing. Being married is safer, Henry. You should think about it. Single guys your age get talked about, whether it's true or not."

"Apparently so."

"People like to talk about other people, it's human nature. And you know what happens when a guy like you gets found out?"

"You mean if they get found out."

"Just a matter of time, the way I see it, Henry. They lose their jobs, they get arrested or put in an institution and diagnosed as diseased with little potential for being cured."

I shuddered. "That could happen to you, too, you know."

"Doubtful. I'm married with a kid. Respectable. I don't mean to scare you, Henry, but I've seen it with single guys. One of the fellows in the Navy, as a matter of fact. He made advances toward the wrong guy in the wrong place one time, and that was it. From what I heard, they put him through some kind of electroshock treatments and finally a lobotomy. You know what that is?"

I nodded, a chill running down my spine.

"Other fellows they castrate or lock away in a psychiatric hospital, never to see the light of day again."

"I've heard stories like that."

"Me too. Wally, the guy from my unit, they tried to get him to talk, I guess. To name names, you know? But he wouldn't do it, even with the electroshock treatments, so I figure if he didn't cave, I never will, either. So you don't have to worry about me, okay?"

I stared at him, still lounging on my bunk, half undressed, still caressing himself, talking about all this, while somewhere back home his wife was probably walking the floor with a crying baby. "So you got married just to protect yourself?"

He shrugged. "Sure, but I like Mary Jane, too. She's a

good egg, we get along real well. You should get married, Heath. It's safer."

"Get married and then sneak around on the side like you do? Why do it at all, Riker? If you're married, just be married. Is all this sneaking about worth the risk?"

"You tell me. Could you stop if you wanted to? I tried, actually, right after Mary Jane and I got hitched. But it didn't last long. Soon I found myself hanging out with the boys down at the gym and sauna. Each time I told myself that was the last time, but I was only fooling myself. You just have to be careful, that's all."

"I understand, Riker, I do. But I don't see how you can face Mary Jane every day, especially after, well, you know."

"She's happy with her life, and I'm happy with mine. Where is there a problem?"

"But you're not being honest with her."

"She loves me. If she knew about my male friends, it would destroy her, ruin her life, her world, everything she knows. She doesn't want that, believe me."

"So you tell yourself."

"So I know. Are you any better, Henry? You're living a lie, too, every day, to everyone: the chief, your folks, your friends, your neighbors..."

"But not to myself. To some degree, we have to lie or hide, for self-preservation, but I don't do it when it hurts someone else."

"I'm not hurting Mary Jane. She's happy. If you're that concerned about it, though, get a lavender marriage. A guy I know did that, and it's worked out well. Hell, supposedly even America's first couple of the theater have a lavender marriage."

"Lavender marriage?"

"Sure. Are you still wet behind the ears? The husband

likes men and the wife likes women. They get married to each other to keep people from talking, but they both have their flings."

"No kidding."

"No kidding. If it works, it works. Marriage is safe, Henry, and it's a dangerous world."

"You sound like my aunt."

"As long as I don't look like her."

I took him all in again, so charming, attractive, seductive. "No, not in the least, and that's the damned problem." I rubbed my eyes. "It's getting late, Riker. I'd better be getting some sleep."

"Good idea. Turn out the lights and undress."

"I meant you should be going back to your cabin. What will the cook say if you come in late?"

"Who cares? I'll tell him I was having a smoke on deck or something. We can make it fast."

"I don't want to make it at all. I'm tired."

He sat up and looked at me. "You sure?"

I thought for only the briefest of moments. "Yeah, I'm sure."

"Suit yourself." He picked his coat up off the floor and slipped it on. "I'm good, you know. When I was finished with you, the neighbors would have needed a cigarette."

"I don't doubt it, but no thanks."

He shrugged. "Okay." He did up his shirt and tie once more before slipping on his shoes as he sat on the edge of the bunk.

I stood up carefully, gripping the edge of the desk, and he followed suit, standing mere inches from me, looking sultry beyond belief.

"If you change your mind, just beep. Beep, beep, beep. Remember, I'm on call." He brought his face closer yet to mine, and I could feel his breath, our noses touching, our lips so close. "I'll leave the tray here until morning, just in case."

Suddenly I remembered the coded letter, still sitting on the desk next to the tray. "I almost forgot, Riker, do you have a match?"

He grinned at me again. "Yes, my lips to yours." I didn't move, partly for fear, partly out of excitement. He kissed me, not torridly as I would have expected, but gently, tenderly, and I felt myself grow more excited.

"That's not what I meant," I said when he finished, almost out of breath.

He smiled. "I know. Here." He extracted a box of matches from his coat pocket. "Keep 'em as a souvenir."

I took them and held them tightly in my hand. "You shouldn't have done that—the kiss, I mean. We're on duty and, technically, I'm your superior."

"Right on both counts, I guess, Detective, but who are you gonna tell? And I already told you I don't kiss and tell, so what's the harm?"

"You'd better go, Riker."

"I can take a hint. But if you find you can't sleep, beep, beep, beep. Was it Mary Jane that made you change your mind?"

"Who said I had made up my mind in the first place?"

"Some things you don't have to say, Heath. You just feel them, sense them, and like I said, you asked for me tonight. You wanted me to come here. Am I wrong?"

I shook my head slowly, looking at him. "No. No, you're not wrong."

"So what was it? The fact we're on duty and you're a detective and I'm just a policeman?"

"You're not just a policeman, Riker. No policeman is just a policeman any more than a detective is just a detective."

"Come again?"

"Just something I was thinking about, something someone said to me."

"Look, it's late, it's just the two of us. I'm here, you're here—why not make the best of it? In the morning, I go back to being Officer Riker, you go back to being Detective Barrington, and no one's the wiser."

I shook my head, still staring at his beautiful face. "I guess maybe I was hoping something would happen, but you're right. I have changed my mind, and I'm not changing it back. I really don't have an answer for you as to why, I really don't. Mary Jane and the baby was a shock, yes, but something else, too. Or maybe someone else."

He cocked his head. "Oh?"

"Just someone back home that I know. Someone waiting for me."

"What they don't know won't hurt them, trust me."

"But it would hurt me, if that makes sense. A wise man once said, why look for silver once you've found gold? It's crazy, I know, but it's just how I am, who I am."

He touched my cheek, ever so gently. "Okay, I guess I understand. I like who you are, Heath. I really do. I think we could be good friends, and I mean to keep in touch when this is all over." He smiled at me and walked somewhat unsteadily to the door before turning. "Sleep well, Mr. Benson." He unlocked and opened the cabin door and glanced out before turning once more and blowing me a kiss and winking. Then, without another word, he stepped into the passage and closed the door behind him.

CHAPTER TWELVE

I stared at the closed door for several minutes, unsure if I had done the right thing or not. I glanced at the matchbox in my hand: "Friends and Lovers Lounge, 186 N Water Street, Milwaukee." *How appropriate*, I thought as I took out a match and burned the letter in the washbasin. When there was nothing left but ashes, I undressed for bed. It was eleven thirty before I doused the light and made an attempt to go to sleep.

The pillow smelled of Riker's hair tonic, and I inhaled it like an elixir before dozing off. I slept fitfully and intermittently, but I remember dreaming that I was with Alan, Riker, and Rosemary, and we were all at the state fair together, waiting to ride the Ferris wheel. Alan and Riker were fighting over who would ride with Rosemary. The three of them got in together, leaving me to ride alone.

I awoke with a jolt and just lay in my bunk, unable to get back to sleep, sweating and feeling the boat heave and roll beneath me. I turned on the small reading light and glanced at my pocket watch in the netting next to my bunk, which told me it was just past two in the morning. I shook my head, rubbing my eyes, and wondered if Alan was asleep back home. Then I guiltily wondered if Riker was.

My eyes adjusted to the light, and I looked around the

small cabin, listening to the boat creak, the engine hum, and the water rushing by outside. I picked up my book from the netting and attempted to read, but I couldn't concentrate. I was wide awake, so I decided to get up, hanging on to the desk to steady myself against the rise and fall. The steward call button on the wall next to the main door seemed to taunt me, urging me to press it three times, beep, beep, beep.

I stood with my finger on the button, so tempted, but I left it be and decided to go up on deck for some fresh air. I wiped the sweat off me and managed to get dressed. I debated putting on my shoulder harness. I never found it comfortable, but I decided better to have it and not need it than need it and not have it. I put my suit coat on but left my fedora on the hook. With a glance in the mirror, I slipped out of my cabin, closing the door quietly behind me.

Holding on to the railing, I made my way down the passage and up the stairs to the boat deck and then outside. The wind slapped me in the face like an ice-cold hand, and the darkness of the night was startling. The running lights had been turned off for the night, and it was black as coal dust, but the moonless sky had cleared and the stars were mesmerizing once my eyes adjusted.

I felt the lake spray, and I estimated we were now in three- to four-foot swells, enough to make standing difficult without hanging on to something. I debated going back inside, but the air was refreshing. I decided to go back to the aft deck, where there would be a break from the wind. It was completely silent except for the hum of the engines and the sound of the water rushing by, and I found it very soothing.

The temperature had dropped to about forty-five degrees, and I knew I wouldn't be able to stay up here too long, but I clung to the rail, staring up at the sky and the stars in awe, feeling humbled and confused. A year ago, a month ago, a

day ago I was far more confident and self-assured. Now I was upside down and inside out over everything. Something about Riker attracted me. Was it his youth? His looks? His manner? I didn't know. He was so different from Alan, and yet they were so alike.

Rosemary was pretty, nice, and smart. Any man would be lucky to have her, and she was clearly interested in me. If only I felt about her the way I did Alan, but I knew from years of trying I couldn't force the issue. Still, maybe Verbina had a point. Perhaps Rosemary and I could be happy together in spite of my feelings. But could I live with myself, sneaking around on her, meeting men for secret rendezvous? And would Rosemary truly be satisfied just being a detective's wife? And did Alan and I have any kind of future together? A life lived in the shadows and lies? Would that be fair to him?

I was lost in my thoughts when I heard scuffling from the starboard side of the boat. I turned in the direction of the noise in time to see what looked like a body go over the railing. I caught a glimpse of black and white, then heard a large splash as whatever or whoever it was hit the water below. I leaned over, but all I saw was blackness as the boat heaved back and forth. I moved quickly along the starboard side, willing my eyes to see into the dark but failing miserably. Was there someone else there too? I couldn't be sure.

I came across a life ring tethered to the side and tossed it overboard, then drew my gun as a precaution. I found nothing as I moved forward, clinging to the rail, until eventually I reached the wheelhouse, illuminated with a soft green glow from the various dials and gauges. I could see Captain Clark through the glass in the door, still standing at the wheel, almost as if he'd never moved since our conversation. Wasting no time on pleasantries, company rules or protocol, I burst into the wheelhouse, the door slamming shut behind me.

"Captain, someone has gone overboard. I was on the aft deck just now and saw a body go over the rail, then I heard a loud splash. It looked like Mr. Slavinsky—at least I think I caught a glimpse of the jacket he wore tonight."

He moved the wheel, beginning the process of turning around. "Are you sure?"

"Definitely. There was a sound of a scuffle on deck, then the splash. I searched briefly but I couldn't find anyone else on deck."

How long ago?"

"No more than just a few minutes, tops. As soon as I heard it, I made my way up here. I threw a life ring over."

"Good thinking." He moved a lever, which I could tell was slowing the engine, and hit a button that turned on a bright spotlight. He punched another button, picked up the telephone, and barked into it. "I need you on deck, Willy. Possible man overboard." He punched a different button and, after a brief pause, said, "Riker, this is the captain. Possible man overboard situation. Check all the cabins and see if anyone's missing. Benson's up here with me." He glanced over at me then and I realized I was still holding my gun, which I quickly put away. "What were you doing out there this time of night anyway, Mr. Benson?"

"I couldn't sleep, thought I'd get some fresh air," I said, holstering my gun.

"Uh-huh. And you carry a gun on your late-night strolls?"

Before I could answer, Willy appeared from the cabin behind the wheelhouse, half-dressed but alert.

"Man the spotlight, Willy. By my calculation, we should be at the spot where Mr. Benson heard the splash." He idled the engine to slow and began making a wide turn. Willy went out on deck and took the spotlight, moving it in an arc back and forth across the water. On his fourth pass, he spotted the life ring I had tossed overboard, bobbing in the waves, but no sign of life. Soon after, Riker appeared from below, looking unkempt but surprisingly calm.

"Everyone accounted for except Mr. Slavinsky, Captain. He's not in his cabin, and I checked the head, the lounge, and the dining room. I had a glance about the decks, too—nothing. I told the other passengers to stay in their cabins."

The captain looked grim. "Search again, Riker, everywhere. Take one of those flashlights and check every corner, every deck, including the hold. Be quick but thorough. I'm going to keep circling."

"Yes, sir." Riker glanced at me, and I nodded. He then grabbed the flashlight and headed out once more.

"Let me help, Captain. I have some experience in this sort of thing."

"I'd appreciate the assistance, Mr. Benson. The water this far out is freezing. If he did go overboard, he won't last long, even if he's a strong swimmer."

I grabbed the other flashlight and cut a swath of light ahead of me, moving it from side to side along the deck. Just past the starboard lifeboat I caught sight of a man's shoe lying just inside the railing. I carefully picked it up and tucked it inside my coat before resuming my search. After ten minutes, I returned to the wheelhouse, the captain steadfastly still circling and Willy still on deck, shivering behind the search lamp as he moved it back and forth, hugging it for warmth.

"I found this on the deck near the starboard lifeboat," I said, pulling the man's shoe from my coat. "Looks like it belongs to a fairly small man. Could be Slavinsky's."

Riker appeared behind me, shaking his head. "He's nowhere to be found, Captain. I even looked inside the lifeboats."

"I found this shoe next to the starboard lifeboat, Riker.

Check his cabin and see if the size matches up to any others he has. Better check on the other cabins again, too. Tell them what's happened and try to keep them below decks and out of the way."

"Yes, sir." Riker took the shoe and headed down to Slavinsky's cabin as the captain looked at me rather strangely.

"I have a history of insurance claim investigations," I said.

"Uh-huh, and a gun." He picked up his radio microphone and turned a dial as it squawked accordingly. "This is the *Speakeasy*, 6255 Alpha Gamma Bravo, calling the Coast Guard, urgent, over." We waited in silence, then he repeated the message.

A staticky voice boomed from the radio. "This is the Coast Guard cutter *Abendera*. What is your emergency? Over."

"Captain Clark of the Great Lakes touring boat *Speakeasy* here. looks like a passenger overboard. I'm circling position and using my spotlight. The boat has been thoroughly searched, one male unaccounted for. Over."

"Roger that, 6255. What is your position?"

The captain gave our position, referring to his log and the charts near him.

"We're an hour south of you, Captain, but on our way, top speed. Let us know if your status changes."

"Roger, *Abendera*. We'll keep circling slowly until you get here. Out." He switched off the microphone. "An hour, son of a bitch." He spat a wad of chewing tobacco into the tin on the floor.

I seconded that expression. I was supposed to babysit Slavinsky and Ballentine, but I blew it. I could reason that Riker blew it, too, but I was the detective on the case, I was in charge, and I had to take full responsibility.

"Did it look like Slavinsky who went over the rail?" the captain asked.

"I think so, maybe. I couldn't tell. It was dark and happened a distance from where I was. It was more a shape than anything, but it looked like a body. As I said, I thought I caught a glimpse of the black and white checked coat Slavinsky was wearing."

"Son of a bitch."

I felt sick to my stomach as I watched the captain staring out into the blackness, continuing to circle. Riker reappeared from the port door. "It's Slavinsky's shoe all right—same size seven as the others in his cabin. And this was on the desk in his cabin…"

He handed me a folded piece of paper, which I read with some difficulty in the dim light: "I can't go on like this. Forgive me, but better to give myself to the cold depths of the lake than to forever be hounded by dogs. G. Slavinsky."

"Suicide?" I said.

"It appears that way, sir."

I took out the card Slavinsky had given me earlier with his sister's name and address on it and compared the handwriting. "It appears to be a perfect match, all right."

"Maybe he gave you his sister's contact information because he planned on jumping overboard."

I turned the note over in my hand before sliding it into my pocket along with the business card. "Maybe. Hounded by dogs. Interesting. Captain, I might as well come clean with you. I'm Detective Barrington of the Milwaukee Police on assignment to watch Gregor Slavinsky, along with Mr. Ballentine and his associate."

"I figured you weren't an insurance man."

"No, sir. I'm sorry for the subterfuge, but we felt it necessary. Riker here is an undercover policeman."

"Son of a bitch. What's this all about? What were you watching him for?"

"It's classified, Captain, but there will be a full investigation."

"Classified, my ass. This is my boat, Detective, and I'm in charge. What the hell is going on? You running around on deck with a gun, a man overboard, undercover police watching my passengers, posing as my steward."

"I wish I could tell you more right now, but I can't."

"Son of a bitch. I wouldn't want to be in your shoes when they find out you lost the fellow you were supposed to be watching. What did he do that you had to watch him? And what did Ballentine do?"

I shook my head. "As I said, there will be a full investigation when we get back to port."

"I need to know if there is any danger to any of my other passengers, crew, or boat, Detective."

"I believe there is no imminent danger, Captain. Again, I apologize for the subterfuge, but my chief felt it necessary."

"Uh-huh. Son of a bitch. You *believe*. That and a nickel will buy me a cup of coffee."

"What happens now?" Riker said.

"Man overboard, presumed drowned—most likely we'll be heading back to Milwaukee once the Coast Guard arrives," the captain said gruffly. "Son of a bitch."

"Why not just continue to Michigan?"

"Milwaukee's the port of call for this vessel, and Slavinsky is from Milwaukee," I said.

"I see," Riker said. "I'd better inform the passengers, then."

"Good idea, Riker. Be sure Slavinsky's cabin is locked and secured, including the connecting door. I don't want anyone in there," I said firmly.

"Yes, sir."

"I think you'd both better get below and stay there until the Coast Guard gets here," the captain growled.

"Aye, Captain." Riker straightened his jacket and headed below. I noted the time was 3:17.

"Captain, I'll need to notify my chief. May I use your ship-to-shore to send a wire?"

"Be my guest, Detective. You're apparently more in charge than I am."

I called Western Union and sent a telegram to Chief Scott. *Boat returning to Milwaukee. Slavinsky overboard. Will contact you once ashore.*

That done, I turned once more to the captain, who was looking grim. "If Slavinsky went overboard, what are the chances of his body being found?"

"Depends, Detective. If he committed suicide, chances are he wouldn't want to be found, so he probably filled his pockets with weights. He'd sink like a rock. This part of the lake is one of the deepest, so it's not very likely we'd find any trace of him."

"Gone, just like that."

"Yup. Not sure how he managed to lose a shoe, though. Sometimes, people jumping overboard take off their shoes to make it easier to swim, but obviously he didn't care about that."

"Maybe it slipped off as he was climbing over the rail."

"Most likely."

"Well, I'll leave you be and go below, Captain. I'll check in once the Coast Guard arrives."

"If you see Riker, tell him I could use some coffee if he still does that sort of thing."

"I think he can manage. I'll let him know."

"Thanks. Son of a bitch."

I went below where I found Ballentine and George in the lounge with Riker, drinks in their hands. "What's this all about, Benson?" Ballentine said. They were both barefoot in their undershirts and trousers.

At that moment, Mr. Whitaker and his aunt entered. They had taken the time to get fully dressed, down to her big hat, gloves, veil, cameo choker and dark glasses, and his fresh sport coat, shirt and tie, though no carnation in the lapel. Mrs. Woodfork must have applied a fresh spritz of violet perfume as well.

"Ah hello, Mr. Whitaker, Mrs. Woodfork. Please join us."

"What's going on? Who put you in charge?"

"Actually, Mr. Ballentine, my boss did. I'm Detective Barrington of the Milwaukee Police. I've been working undercover along with Officer Riker here to watch Mr. Slavinsky."

"What the hell are you talking about?"

"Huh?" George added.

"It's a long story, but Mr. Slavinsky has gone overboard. We're circling trying to find him, and the Coast Guard is on the way to assist. Most likely, we will be returning to Milwaukee."

"Riker mentioned about Mr. Slavinsky, but must we really return to Milwaukee? That is most inconvenient, Mr. Benson," Mr. Whitaker said.

"It's Detective Barrington. I'm sorry, but your inconvenience versus a man's life is not exactly equal in my book, Mr. Whitaker," I snapped. "Oh, and Riker, the captain wants coffee. I could use some, too. Do you mind?"

Riker shrugged. "I guess I'm still on duty. Anyone else?"

"I'll stick to bourbon," Ballentine said.

"Thank you, no," Whitaker said, speaking for both himself and his aunt. He looked quite upset and agitated.

"I'm good, thanks," George said.

"Back in a moment, then."

"I suggest you all go back to your cabins. There's nothing to see or do here. Once the Coast Guard arrives, we'll probably start back."

"I'm more comfortable here, Detective. So is George."

"Well, we're going back to bed. My aunt needs her rest, and this is all most discomforting."

"Good idea, Mr. Whitaker. You look rather unwell yourself."

"Indeed, this is all most distressing. Come, Auntie." He held out his arm once more, and she took it gingerly. "I expect a full reimbursement of our tickets since we are returning to Milwaukee."

"You can take that up with the owners of the *Speakeasy*, Mr. Whitaker."

"Indeed I shall." The two of them exited the lounge and headed slowly back to their cabin.

"That dandy is something else. A full refund indeed," Ballentine said.

"Mr. Slavinsky's disappearance is a far greater concern right now, Mr. Ballentine."

"I would agree with you there. Have you searched the whole boat? You sure he's not still on board?"

"You tell me, Mr. Ballentine."

"Me? How should I know?"

"You certainly had a motive to get rid of Mr. Slavinsky."

"You mean because of our little business deal?"

"I do, and about your past history with Slavinsky. I've done my research. There's a whole file on you two at the station, you know."

He laughed again. "I figured as much. You didn't seem much like an insurance salesman, though I commend you on a valiant effort. The business cards were a nice touch."

"Thanks."

"But you're dead wrong—pardon the expression—about me having a motive to bump off Gregor. We were friends."

"Right, pals," I said sarcastically.

"Besides, he hadn't paid back the money yet. Why would I do him in before I get my cash back?"

"Good question. Maybe he told you where the money is, so you had no further use for him."

"Fat chance. Slavinsky's not stupid, Detective, or at least he wasn't."

"He also didn't seem like the type to commit suicide, Ballentine."

"Eh, don't surprise me. Gregor was in over his head again, and he didn't have me to bail him out this time. He was a weak, lazy coward."

"You do indeed sound like good friends."

"We go way back. We just went in different directions. I'm a legitimate businessman now, ain't I, George?"

"Yes, sir." George nodded agreeably.

"I don't go bumping people off anymore, Detective. Not that I'm saying I ever did."

"No, I imagine you have people for that."

"Funny guy," he snarled.

Riker returned with my coffee, and I took it from him gratefully. "Did you give the captain his?"

"Yes, he's all set. I brought one for Willy, too. He was freezing out on deck. The Coast Guard is about ten minutes away. They made better time than they thought."

"Good." I turned back to Ballentine. "When and where did you last see Slavinsky, Mr. Ballentine?"

"Right here in the lounge when he said good night, same as you."

"Same here," George said.

"I don't know what you hoped to achieve out here, watching over us, playing games, lying to us."

"It was an assignment, Mr. Ballentine. Confidential."

"Yeah, well, it's over, done, finished, just like Slavinsky. I wash my hands of him, take a loss, write it off."

"Just like that?"

He shrugged. "Got any better ideas? The louse had no friends and no family except for his sister and aunt, and they sure don't have twenty-five grand lying around."

"We're not through with you, Mr. Ballentine. Not just yet."

"I think you are. And if you have any more questions for me, you can save them for my attorneys."

"I'm sure you have plenty of them on your payroll, too. I guess I'm through with you for now, then. Let's get back up to the wheelhouse, Riker. The Coast Guard should be here by this time."

"Stay away from the railing, Detective. The decks can get slippery in rough seas, and it's easy to fall overboard. You don't want to go keeping Slavinsky company."

"Is that a threat, Ballentine?"

"Just a friendly warning."

"Fair enough. I'd advise the two of you to get some sleep. I'll have more questions in the morning once we dock."

"Like I said, Detective, I ain't answering any more questions, now or in the morning. Unless you can come up with a reason to arrest me, I'll bid you two good night. Come on, George. We've got packing to do." He slammed down the rest of his drink, stood up and left the lounge, George following dutifully behind.

CHAPTER THIRTEEN

Riker and I made our way to the bridge, where the Captain stood by the wheel, sipping his coffee. Through the windows, I could see the lights of the cutter *Abendera* keeping a wide berth from us just off the port bow.

"What's the status, Captain?"

"I gave them all the information I had. They're going to continue searching the waters while we head back to Milwaukee. Nothing else, unless you have anything you're not telling me."

I shook my head. "No, that covers it. Again, my apologies for keeping you in the dark. What time do you think we'll reach port?"

He glanced at a clock on the wall. "Best guess about seven. The wind seems to be dying down and the lake is calming. We'll be under way shortly. The Coast Guard said they will have a police car meet us at the pier."

"Right. Well, we might as well pack our things and see if we can get an hour or two's rest, then."

"Might as well. I sent Willy back to bed a while ago. I'll stay up here until we reach port."

Riker and I went below deck. At the top of the stairs, he paused. "Not exactly the way we expected this to turn out, is it, Detective?"

"No, not exactly, Riker."

"I'm sorry about what happened. I mean with Slavinsky and everything. I was out of bounds."

"Not your fault, Riker."

"Not yours either, Detective. You did everything right. You made all the right calls."

"I wish I could be as sure. And it is my fault. I was in charge."

"You still are, sir. You're a fine detective."

"Thanks. Get some rest. I'll try and do the same."

Riker nodded. "Right. See you in a few hours." I watched him as he went down the stairs to the crew quarters. When he was gone, I made my way back to cabin four. Alone with my thoughts, my head ached. I replayed the night's events again in my mind as I packed my belongings and at last stretched out on the bunk and closed my eyes.

CHAPTER FOURTEEN

We docked in Milwaukee just after seven, the sun glowing bright on the eastern horizon over the lake. I had slept fitfully and now pulled myself out of the bunk and dressed in my clothes from the night before, forgoing a shower. I climbed out on deck where Riker was waiting, still in his uniform looking remarkably fresh.

"Good morning, sir."

"Good morning, Riker. It comes awfully early, doesn't it?"

"Yes, sir. Coffee? I brewed a fresh pot just a bit ago."

I looked blankly at him. "Did you get any sleep at all? You do realize your duties as cabin steward are over, right?"

He shrugged. "Yes, but I figured you may need some coffee. The cook actually made it. I just brought it up here." He poured from a metal carafe on a stand near the stairway entrance. "Black, just the way you like it, Heath."

I wrapped my hands around the mug, feeling the warmth, breathing in the aroma. "Thanks, you really are something. Where are the others?"

"Ballentine and George are in the lounge, Mrs. Woodfork and Mr. Whitaker are still in their cabin. I offered to help with their luggage, but they said they could manage. Mr. Whitaker still seems quite annoyed and upset by all this."

"Understandably so."

I looked over the railing at the dock, where a black-and-white was waiting for us. Taking another gulp of the coffee, I turned back to Riker. "I guess I'd better disembark and get things going. Thanks again for the coffee, I needed that." I handed him back the mug, which he set on the tray.

"My pleasure, sir. What happens next?"

"I'd appreciate it if you stay aboard for a while. I want the boat searched one more time, and I could use your assistance."

"At your service, Detective." Riker grinned.

I returned his smile. "I'm sure. You can let the others off once I finish talking to the officers on the dock." I walked down the gangway to the dock, feeling a bit unsteady and woozy as I had to adjust to being on land. I spoke to the two officers, briefing them on what had happened, and then I gave a nod to Riker on deck. Shortly after, Ballentine and George disembarked looking tired and mean, lugging their bags under their arms. I couldn't think of anything to detain them for, and they refused to answer any more questions without a lawyer present.

Mr. Whitaker and Mrs. Woodfork came off last, looking much the worse for wear. She was still dressed in her mourning attire, and I couldn't help but wonder why she bothered to pack a bag at all.

"Good morning," I said, though clearly it wasn't.

"Good only to be back on dry land, I would say," Whitaker responded.

"Yes, I'm sorry things didn't work out as planned."

He laughed. "A cramped tiny boat, awful food, large waves, and then on top of it all, being wakened in the middle of the night by a man overboard? What could be better? And then ending up back where we started twelve hours earlier. I expect a full refund, along with a letter of apology."

"I do apologize. As for the refund, you'll have to take that up with the boat's owners."

"I'm feeling rather unwell. We should go," Mrs. Woodfork said, her voice so soft and raspy, I had to strain to hear her words. The scent of violet perfume still hung about her.

"You see how upsetting this has been?" Whitaker asked.

"Does your aunt need a doctor?"

"No. We need to be left alone, on dry, non-moving land."

"May we arrange transportation back to Chicago?"

"I appreciate that you are trying to make up for a horrible night, Detective, but your assistance is not required. The captain has graciously radioed and made overnight accommodations for us here in Milwaukee at the Water's Edge motel. Tomorrow we're taking a train to upper Michigan."

"I imagine you'll find the train more relaxing."

"A train to Michigan is indeed a welcome change from a rocky boat to Michigan, Mr. Benson, or Detective Barrington, or whatever your name is."

"It was not my nor the police department's intention to disrupt your plans, folks. I hope your train trip is more relaxing."

"As do we. Good day." I watched them meander down the pier, Whitaker struggling under the weight of his and her bags and Mrs. Woodfork leaning on his arm. Mrs. Woodfork, I noticed, carried the carpetbag with her medicine in one of her small, gloved hands. If they made it to the taxi without dropping anything or dropping over, I'd be amazed.

I motioned for the two officers who had been standing by. "We need to do a thorough search of the boat, every square inch. I want to make sure Slavinsky did indeed go overboard and isn't actually hiding somewhere."

"Yes, sir," the younger one said.

"Riker and I searched last night, but I want to be absolutely certain we didn't miss anything. I'll give you a hand. Officer Riker is still on board and knows the boat fairly well. He'll be our guide below decks."

"Whatever you say, Detective. Will we need a search warrant?"

I shook my head. "The captain is cooperating and allowing us to have a look around, fortunately. I think he just wants to be done with us as soon as possible and on his way."

"Understood."

The three of us climbed aboard and, together with Riker, we turned over every inch of that tug, including my cabin and the crew's quarters, much to the captain's chagrin. He had quite an interesting collection of reading material. Clearly he and Ballentine had at least one thing in common. Besides that and some forgotten hooch probably left over from Prohibition twenty years earlier that we found stashed inside a vent pipe, we found nothing of interest. Certainly no trace of Slavinsky.

I gave up, convinced that Slavinsky was not hiding on board. "All right, boys, I guess that's it, then. I'm finished here."

"Yes, sir. I think we covered every inch except Mr. Slavinsky's cabin."

"Riker and I searched that ourselves earlier, but it wouldn't hurt to have one more look. I had it locked as a precaution."

The four of us went below again to the cabins, and Riker unlocked Slavinsky's door. I glanced inside the small space. His suitcase was still tucked beneath the bunk, his toiletries still near the sink, his bunk undisturbed. "It looks like he never went to bed."

"A troubled soul. Probably couldn't sleep, making up his mind to end it all."

"Sad. He didn't seem to have much of a life, you know?"

"He made some bad choices, had some bad breaks," I said.

"I want all of his possessions inventoried and documented before being removed and stored, and a full set of photos taken, just in case. Radio for a team from the lab for that, will you?"

"Yes, sir." The older policeman nodded and headed down the corridor to the gangway to his squad.

"Anything else for me, Detective?" the younger officer asked, bright eyed and eager.

"No, not at the moment. Thanks for your help. You two can get back to your patrol."

"Yes, sir. Thank you, sir." I smiled as I watched him walk down the hall as well, following his partner. When they had both gone, I turned to Riker.

"Lock this room up again and stay in the hall until the boys from the lab get here. When they do, I'm putting you in charge. Oversee the inventory process and make sure nothing is overlooked. I'll make my report to the chief."

"Yes, sir."

"Have them take his belongings downtown when they've finished and give them to the sergeant for storage. His aunt and sister will need to be notified once his death has been confirmed, and then they can claim the items. And I'll want a copy of the inventory. Be sure and inventory everything, no matter how minute or seemingly trivial."

"I will, sir. What should I do afterward? I'm still on the clock, you know," Riker said.

"Check in with headquarters downtown. I can't think of anything else here at the moment, and depending on what the chief says, there may not be anything more anywhere, at least not in regard to this case."

"I understand. At least it will be nice to get out of this monkey outfit and back into uniform."

I laughed. "It will be a while before the lab boys get here. Come help me with my bag, if you don't mind."

"Yes, sir." He and I stepped across the passage into my room, where I had pretty much packed everything up already. The tea tray still sat on the desk.

"I guess I should take that back to the galley, sir," Riker said.

"Yeah, I guess so. I just need to get my hat." I grabbed it from its hook as Riker picked up my suitcase. "I was only kidding about carrying my bag."

"I don't mind, Detective. I've been working all day and night. I'll come back for the tea tray."

"You did get the worst of it this trip, Riker."

He shrugged. "It's okay. Part of the job. I'm sorry again if I let you down."

"You didn't. Neither of us could have predicted what happened out there. And if Slavinsky really wanted to kill himself, he would have found a way to do it no matter how much we tried to watch him."

"I suppose. The whole thing is strange, though. You did everything you could, sir."

"Thanks. Let's hope the chief agrees."

"Fingers crossed. So, what happens after all this?"

"You finish your shift, and then you go home to your wife and kid and get some rest. As I said, I have reports to fill out and the chief to answer to."

"That really bothers you, doesn't it?"

"What? Answering to the chief?"

"No, Mary Jane and my kid."

"They don't bother me, but they should bother you."

"I meant what I said before. I like you, and I think we could be friends."

"Maybe, but just friends. You've got your life to live, and I've got mine."

"If that's the way you want it."

"That's the way it has to be. I'll make sure you get a full recommendation for your part in all this."

"You'd do that? Even after what happened?"

"Nothing happened, except Slavinsky jumped overboard. You did your job and you did it well. It will all be in my report. Nothing else."

"Thanks, Detective. I really appreciate that. If you think of something else for me to do, just call."

"Thanks, I will. You have a sharp mind, and your knowledge and memory may still come in handy. I'd appreciate it, though, if the next time the guys start talking about me you put in a good word."

He grinned at me. "You got it. Good luck with the chief. I don't envy you."

"Thanks. I'd better send a wire and let him know we're back. I'm sure he'll want to see me right away."

"Yeah, I suppose so." We climbed the stairs and walked to the gangplank.

"All right, I can take my bag from here. Call me if you or the boys from the lab find anything we overlooked the first time."

"Will do. See you around, Detective."

"See you, Riker."

"Oh, and Detective?"

"Yes?"

"That other person, the one waiting for you—they're pretty lucky."

I smiled. "Thanks. I hope they think so."

I climbed down the gangplank and stood on the pier, watching him walk away down the deck, still admiring the view. I picked up my suitcase and headed out. A Western Union counter was just inside the main pier building, so I sent a cable to the chief, letting him know I'd be at the station at ten. It was just after nine. I knew he was expecting a full report, and I wasn't looking forward to it. I knew he wouldn't be happy. I hoped he was able to get his screens in and had gotten a better night's sleep. After sending the wire, I decided to go back to my apartment for a shower, shave, and change of clothes. Once I got out of the shower and got dressed again, I felt only mildly refreshed. I padded over to the phone in the hall and dialed the station downtown. "Hey, Bennett, it's Barrington. Messages?"

"And how. The chief wants to see you in his office first thing this morning."

"What's first thing?"

"It's a Friday and a holiday, so who knows? But I'd get your ass down here right away if I were you, it's coming ten already."

"Did he get my telegram?"

"He didn't say. He got in about half an hour ago, and he didn't look happy."

"Roger that, Bennett. Thanks." I hung up and dialed Alan's place. The phone rang six, then seven times before Alan picked up. "Hello?" He sounded groggy.

"Hey, sleepyhead, it's almost ten. What are you doing still in bed?"

"Heath! I didn't expect to hear from you this morning. The stag party went late, I'm beat."

"Have a good time?"

"Okay. You in Michigan?"

"No. I'm back home in Milwaukee."

"Oh? Really? What happened?"

"Long story. I have to meet the chief down at the station, which should be a real gas. Want to meet for lunch later?"

Pause. "I have the day off, remember? I was going to go check out the tennis match down at the lake later."

"I see."

"What's up with your case?"

"Things have taken an unexpected turn, and I could use your help. I'm going to ask the chief if I can get you assigned to me temporarily."

"You really think I can help you?"

"You always have in the past. I really missed you, Alan."

"I just saw you yesterday, Heath."

"I know, it's stupid. *I'm* stupid."

"No arguments there."

"Thanks. I'm sorting through a lot of stuff, Alan. Be patient with me, please?"

"I'm a patient kind of guy. I just like to know where I stand."

"At the front of the line, believe me. I know that more than ever now. Meet me for lunch?"

Pause. "I can be downtown at noon. I'll meet you at Schwimmer's."

"Perfect."

"Hopefully, I'll live up to your expectations and be of some help."

"Believe it or not, Alan, I like you for more than your handsome face and body. I like to bounce ideas off you. And you always give me solid dick, you don't sugarcoat things."

"Well, thanks. Look, Heath, it's been a crazy few months since we met, and I know we're both still sorting things out..."

"Yeah?"

"Yeah, well, like you said, I give you solid dick, so here goes. I like you a lot, more than I ever expected to. I understand that your job is important to you, and I'm glad that you like to share it with me. I just want to know that if push came to shove, you'd choose me."

"Alan, believe me, I already chose you. And that's solid

dick, no fooling. I'm sorry now I ever agreed to take this assignment. Oh, how I wish we'd gone fishing."

"That makes two of us. I'll see you at noon, Detective. Should I be in uniform?"

"I hate to spoil your day off, but you will be on duty if the chief agrees."

"Great, just great. Remind me again why I like you."

"Because I'm smart, charming, witty, and attractive."

"You left out humble."

I laughed. "See you at noon, Officer."

I hung up the phone, grabbed my hat and coat, and headed downstairs.

I was at the station by almost ten. Kunkel was at the desk, filling in for Sukawaty, whose wife just had a baby. "Morning, Detective."

"Morning, Kunkel."

"You look like death warmed over. You been up all night?"

"Something like that, and nice to see you, too. The chief ready for me?"

"And how, but he wants your report first, so you'd better get cracking. What the hell happened? He is none too happy."

"It's a long story. At least the heat wave finally broke."

"Small comfort."

"Some comfort is better than none. Maybe he slept better last night."

"Not from the looks of him. You'd better get upstairs. That report's not going to type itself, you know."

"Right. If you hear screaming later, send reinforcements."

Kunkel laughed. "Want me to sign you in?"

"No, I'm not here officially. I'll let you know if things change."

"Your funeral."

"Let's hope not."

"I'll send flowers."

"Funny." I went upstairs to my desk in the detectives' room, where I uncovered the typewriter and set to work. Only a few people milled about, and I was glad for the privacy. I didn't need or want a lot of questions right now. I didn't have any answers, anyway.

At ten thirty, Kunkel called. "The chief just called down. He wants you in his office in fifteen minutes. You finished?"

"With the report, yes. Hopefully, not with the force."

"Wowzer, you must have done something all right or all wrong."

"Yeah, one of those two. Thanks." I hung up and read through my report briefly. I noticed a few mistakes, but I didn't have time to correct them. I covered my typewriter again and tidied up my already tidy desk, then used the bathroom to dispose of my morning coffee. I knocked lightly on the glass in the chief's door with a minute to spare. "What?" he responded in his gruff voice. I opened the door and went inside, closing it behind me.

The chief was pacing back and forth behind his desk.

"Good morning," I volunteered. From the looks of his ashtray, he'd already burned through two cigarettes.

"You have your report?"

"Yes, sir. Right here." I held it out for him, but he didn't take it. I dropped it on the desk and waited.

"I don't like coming downtown on a holiday, Barrington. I had promised the missus we'd go to the zoo in Washington Park today. She likes the monkeys, you know."

"I'm sorry, Chief."

"What do you have against monkeys?"

"No, I mean I'm sorry you had to come down here. I like monkeys, too."

"You're sorry all right. A sorry detective, and you look like hell. Not like you at all."

"I didn't get much sleep, and you wanted to see me right away."

"Damned right I did. I got your wire at five in the morning. Scared the hell out of my wife, Western Union ringing the bell at that time of day. Our nephew is still overseas, you know, in the Army. Then I had to contact the FBI and tell them the boat had returned to Milwaukee and Slavinsky drowned, for Christ's sake. They want to know what the hell happened, and so do I. They'll want to see your report, too, so I hope it's complete."

"A few typos, but otherwise as thorough as I can make it, sir."

"I don't give a shit about typos, Barrington. All you had to do was keep an eye on Slavinsky and Ballentine, and you blew it."

I swallowed and felt about six inches tall. "Yes, sir, I did."

He continued pacing back and forth, pausing only to light a third cigarette. "You're a good detective, Barrington, a good cop. How did this happen? Was it Riker?"

I shrank to about four inches. "Was what Riker, sir?"

"Was this his fault? He's fairly new on the force. Did you ask him to watch Slavinsky while you kept an eye on Ballentine?"

"No, sir. Riker did his job and did it well. I take full responsibility for what happened, or didn't happen, in watching Slavinsky."

He stopped by the window and stared out, blowing smoke. "I figured you'd say that, and I'm glad you did. I like you, Barrington. Like I said, you're a good cop. But I like the zoo, too, damn it, and this goddamned heat seems to have finally broken."

"Yes, sir."

"You should know Riker was already here this morning."
I looked at him quizzically. "Here?"

"That's right. That's why I kept you waiting. He finished that inventory job you gave him, and he hustled his ass down here to see me."

"I see," I stated, feeling somewhat apprehensive.

"He wanted to get to me before you did. He said you did a first-rate job, and that if anyone was to blame, it was him for distracting you, even though you wouldn't let yourself be distracted, whatever the hell that means. He said he was chatting you up about his wife and kid, but you kept him on track and on the case. He said he admires you a lot, and that you did a first-rate job."

"Very kind of him, sir. It really wasn't any kind of distraction at all. He's a good cop and will make a top-notch detective someday."

"The mutual admiration society." He paced for several minutes, not saying anything, before facing me head-on. "I guess the monkeys can wait until tomorrow. Police work doesn't keep to a schedule, as you know."

"Very true, Chief."

He stubbed out the cigarette in the ashtray next to the other two and looked back at me again. "All right, I'll read your report later, but tell me honestly what happened out there. How in the hell did Slavinsky manage to throw himself overboard without you or Riker noticing?"

I grew a few inches. "Actually I did notice, sir. I was on deck when it happened, around two this morning. I couldn't sleep. It's all in the report."

He rubbed his eyes, and his bushy brows came together like a caterpillar. "I'm sure it is, double spaced just the way

I like it, typos and all. So you couldn't sleep—what then, Barrington?"

I relayed the facts as best I could, leaving out the sordid details of the meeting in my cabin between Riker and myself.

The chief opened his cigarette case and took out a fourth cigarette, turned it over in his hand, and then put it back. "Doris thinks I should quit. She says it stinks up the house, and I also burned a hole in the dining room table last week."

"Ouch."

"Yeah, I'll be paying for that one for a long time. Any reason to believe it wasn't suicide, Barrington?"

"No logical reason. He had a motive. He was heavily in debt to Ballentine, as we know, and he knew Ballentine would kill him in a much less pleasant way than drowning if he didn't make good. He left that note in his cabin, and he did write out his sister's contact information. I passed that along to the sergeant downstairs to get in touch with her. She and an aunt are all the family he had. Fletch in the lab is analyzing the handwriting now to confirm it matches with the note."

"You're sure he didn't just fake the suicide and hide on board somewhere?"

"That was one of my first thoughts, but I saw a body go overboard, and we searched the boat thoroughly. Once we docked, Riker and I searched it again with two other officers. We turned up nothing, and we even looked in the ballast tanks."

"If he went overboard, could he have been picked up by another boat that he'd arranged to rendezvous with?"

"That thought crossed my mind, too, Chief, but it doesn't seem possible. We were in three- and four-foot swells, and the water was near freezing. He wouldn't have lasted long out there, and no other boat was in sight. Just minutes after I saw the body go over, the captain turned around and started searching with a spotlight."

"Damn. So, that's it, then. Sounds pretty open and shut, Barrington. I think you did all you could under the circumstances. Now I just have to get the Feds to believe it. Anyway, at least we don't have to worry about Slavinsky anymore. He's out of our hands and with the devil."

"I suppose so."

"You sound doubtful."

I shrugged. "I really don't know what to believe, Chief. I think it bears more investigating. He didn't seem like the suicide type."

"There is no type when it comes to suicide. He probably wasn't planning on killing himself. We know now he had planned to escape into Canada, but when Ballentine showed up he felt trapped like a rat on that boat, knew Ballentine would follow him anywhere he went, so he decided to end it all. I say we file Gregor Slavinsky under deceased and move along."

"I guess so, but what became of the twenty-five grand? That's what doesn't make sense to me. If he still had the money, why kill himself, Chief? Why not take his chances on still slipping away from Ballentine?"

"What if he blew it all and didn't have it? He'd definitely want to make a run for Canada then."

"True, but what did he blow it on? Or is it still stashed somewhere? Maybe Ballentine coerced him into telling him where it is, and then they bumped him off? They could have forced him at gunpoint to write that suicide note."

"Possible, I suppose."

"I think it bears more investigating," I said.

"What's to investigate? There's no body, no evidence of a crime, nothing, unless you can turn up the money. And even then, it belongs to Ballentine. We can't legally hold it unless you can prove he did bump Slavinsky off, and that doesn't seem likely."

I shook my head. "You're right, but I don't know, sir. I can't put this to bed just yet. I need a little time and some help from an officer."

"Time costs the taxpayers money, Barrington, and I don't see the point. Harass Ballentine, and he'll have his army of lawyers on us."

"I don't plan on harassing him, sir, but there are unanswered questions."

"Such as?"

"I don't know yet. When I know the questions, perhaps I'll know the answers."

"You're talking in riddles. This seems open and shut. You were assigned to watch Slavinsky, he killed himself, your assignment is over. There is no more case, regardless of what he did or didn't do with the money."

"Maybe. But give me one more day to see if I can dig anything else up, please. I have a feeling."

"You sound like my wife—Doris is always having feelings about something." He chewed his lip and fiddled with his cigarette case again, turning it over and over. "All right, Barrington, one day. It's against my better judgment, but I'll give you twenty-four hours, no more. If you don't turn up anything by then, we're done and you can get back to your larceny case."

"Fair enough, Chief. What about a police officer to assist me?"

"Riker would be the obvious choice. He's already familiar with the situation so far, and I guess I could spare him. He's on the case until Sunday anyway."

"Riker performed his job admirably, sir. You chose well for that assignment. But right now I need someone I'm experienced working with to bounce some ideas off of."

"Like who?"

"Alan Keyes, sir."

"The officer who helped you with your last two big cases."

"Yes. I'd like him assigned to me."

"You'd have to check with the sergeant. I don't know his duty roster. If he's available I'll okay it." He scribbled something on to a pad and handed the paper to me. "Give this to Schmidt downstairs. He can see about getting Keyes assigned to you temporarily if he's available."

"Yes, sir, thank you, sir. Oh, and you can have your ring back. The missus and I have officially broken up." I grinned as I pulled the gold band off my finger and handed it to him.

"Thanks. Turn the rest of the documents in to Shirley. She keeps track of all that."

"Will do, Chief."

"By the way, Riker's waiting downstairs for you. See if you can find something for him to help you with. I like his eagerness."

"Understood, sir. Good luck with the Feds, and enjoy the zoo tomorrow."

"Monkeys."

I smiled as I walked out of his office and headed back to my desk. The chief was tough, but fair. I had one day from now to come up with something, and I was completely unsure of what to do next. It was just past eleven, so I went downstairs and found Schmidt. He was none too happy with having to find a last-minute replacement for Keyes on the night shift tomorrow, plus overtime for today, since it was supposed to be Alan's day off.

"The chief approved this, Barrington?"

"You got his note right there, but feel free to check with him if you think I faked it. I'll warn you, the chief's not in the best of moods right now."

"So I heard. This means a mountain of paperwork for me, you know."

"Sorry, Schmidt. I'll make it up to you."

"Get me tickets to the Brewers opener."

"Just do your job, and I'll see what I can do."

He growled at me and I growled back, until he finally handed over the approval slip, which I took to Agnes in payroll. I found Riker nursing a cup of coffee in the lounge.

"Hello, Officer."

He looked up at me, then smiled and got to his feet. "Detective."

"Thanks for what you said to the chief upstairs, but it wasn't necessary. I can handle myself."

He shrugged. "I didn't say anything that wasn't true, more or less, anyway."

"Right. Well, we still have a case to work on, at least for the next twenty-four hours."

"Really?"

"Yup, the chief is letting me have one full day to see if I can come up with something, anything, to either prove Slavinsky killed himself or that he was killed by someone else."

"I don't see how you're going to do that, sir."

I shook my head. "Nor do I. I haven't the slightest idea, but we have to start somewhere. I want you to take an unmarked and head over to Ballentine's house. Be discreet, but keep an eye on any comings and goings. If Ballentine leaves, follow him, but from a safe distance."

"Yes, sir, I'm on it."

"Good. Check in later. Right now I've got a lunch date with Officer Keyes to go over a few other ideas."

"Yes, sir. And Heath? Thanks."

I smiled. "Don't let me down."

CHAPTER FIFTEEN

Schwimmer's was on the corner of Seventh and Wells, a small place not far from the station and an easy walk, popular with the guys on the force. Keyes was already in a booth near the back when I arrived, looking sharp in his uniform, as always. He grinned when he saw me, and I smiled back as I slid in across from him, hanging my fedora from the hook at the end of the booth next to his uniform cap.

"Hey, you."

He gave me a smile. "Hey, Detective. Doesn't look like the chief beat you up too badly."

"I survived, at least so far. I expected far worse. I'm hoping my instincts are right and there's more to this case then meets the eye."

"I'm intrigued. Did he clear me to work with you?"

I nodded. "Yes, you're all mine, at least for the next twenty-four hours, so you're officially on the payroll. Consider this a working lunch."

He laughed. "Nice."

I flipped open the menu and gave it a glance. "What are you having, Keyes?"

"Coffee and the soup. It's chicken noodle, the fifteen cent special."

"We're on the department's dime, indulge yourself."

He grinned at me. "Fair enough. I'll have the baked halibut with mushrooms, that's a dollar forty."

"Let's make it two." I motioned for the waiter, an older, sour-looking fellow whose name tag read Norman. He sauntered over with a pitcher of water.

"Yes, gentlemen?"

"Two black coffees, and two baked halibuts with mushrooms, please."

"Good choice," he replied without the slightest hint of emotion. Norman took our menus and tucked them under his arm as he strolled off to the kitchen, the water pitcher jostling about in his left hand.

"Charming fellow."

"Yes, good thing we're not in a hurry. I get the feeling speed is not his specialty."

"The food's supposed to be good here, though."

"At these prices, I should hope so."

Two black coffees appeared shortly, courtesy of a busboy who looked older than the waiter.

I spooned a bit of ice from my water into the cup to cool it, and Keyes did the same.

"So, since this is a working lunch, fill me in."

"I barely know where to begin, Keyes. You're aware, of course, that I was assigned to go to Mackinac on a boat."

"Yeah, and I guess it got cut short."

"I was supposed to be watching Gregor Slavinsky and Ballentine."

"The gangsters? I thought Slavinsky was in prison."

"He got out this past February."

"Those two are pretty heavy around Milwaukee, Heath. What do you mean, you were supposed to be watching them?"

"It's complicated. Slavinsky booked passage on a boat up to Mackinac, as did Ballentine and his thug George."

"Interesting."

"Slavinsky borrowed somewhere in the neighborhood of twenty-five grand from Ballentine a few months ago, and Ballentine wanted it back."

Keyes whistled. "Twenty-five thousand dollars would buy a lot of baked halibut with mushrooms."

"Indeed. Anyway, the chief figured Ballentine might try something with Slavinsky, maybe coerce him to pay back the money since Slavinsky was behind on his payments. We found out Slavinsky was planning on slipping away to Canada, so he wanted me to watch over them."

"But wouldn't that be more the FBI's department? Crossing state lines and all?"

"That's what I said, but no crime had been committed. It was all speculation, so I was more or less just along to babysit. They even had an undercover cop by the name of Grant Riker posing as a steward. Know him?"

"Name doesn't ring a bell, but I've probably seen him. So it was you, the cop, and the three of them?"

"There was a guy and his elderly aunt on board, too—Mr. Whitaker and Mrs. Woodfork. I felt sorry for them. Their trip was pretty much ruined."

"What happened?"

"Slavinsky went overboard."

"What?" His eyebrows shot up in surprise.

I nodded. "Yup, at around two this morning. As luck would have it, I couldn't sleep and I was up on deck when it happened."

"You saw him jump over?"

"I saw something go over. It looked like a body, and I

caught a glimpse of Slavinsky's black and white plaid sport coat. Plus Slavinsky turned up missing, so two and two equals four, you know?"

"Wowzer."

"Yeah. I found his shoe on deck, too, near the spot that I saw it happen. It must have slipped off when he jumped. He left a note I'm having analyzed to make sure it matches with something he wrote earlier and gave me."

"What did he write earlier?"

"His sister's contact information, on the pretense that she would be a good candidate for insurance."

"Huh?"

"Oh, yeah, I forgot to mention I was undercover as a salesman for Granite Insurance."

"I could see you as an insurance agent, Heath."

"Ballentine couldn't. I guess I wasn't all that convincing. Anyway, Slavinsky gave me his sister's contact information and asked me to call her when we got to shore. He gave it to me just hours before he went over, so it seems likely he really intended it to be more of a final thing."

"Jeepers, so he did commit suicide?"

"It certainly seems like he didn't expect to make it off that boat alive."

"Yeah, it seems that way. What did the note say?"

"Something about 'I can't go on like this, better to give myself to the depths of the lake than to be hounded by dogs.' The dogs being Ballentine and George, presumably. I gave everything to Fletch at the station to analyze and check fingerprints."

"That sure sounds like a final notice. If it's his handwriting, I don't see how it could not be suicide, Heath."

I shrugged and took a sip of my coffee. "I don't either, and neither does the chief. I'm just going on a feeling."

"Yeah, but like you said, two plus two equals four no matter how you add it up."

"You know me, Alan. I never was very good at math."

The waiter arrived at long last with our lunches, and we said nothing for a while as we ate.

"Good choice on the halibut, Keyes."

"Yeah, it's not half bad. Beats chicken noodle soup."

I laughed. "By the way, how was Haffensteffer's big stag party?" I said, draining the remains of my cup and slipping off my left shoe, which had been pinching.

Keyes groaned. "It was okay. The usual, you know? Too many cigars, too many beers, too many slaps on the back."

"You said it was a late night."

He nodded. "Does it show?"

I laughed. "Only a little, and my early morning wakeup call probably didn't help. I'm sure I look worse than you, though. I've been up since about two, and I didn't get much sleep before that."

"Your eyes are a nice shade of red. We're a weary pair, Heath."

I smiled. "I guess so. Did you have a good time, at least?" I playfully ran my left foot on top of his right, knowing no one could see beneath the tablecloth.

He smiled coyly. "I'm having a better time right now, Detective. As for the stag party, remind me not to go to any more of those. They put me in charge of the music, which basically meant I sat next to the phonograph and changed the records all night."

"Fun," I said sarcastically, letting my foot travel up inside his uniform pant leg a bit.

Keyes grinned at me. "I don't think I've ever been frisked by a foot before."

"Always good to try new things, Alan."

"So many things to try. Uh, what was I saying?"

"You were in charge of the music."

"Oh, right. I wish records would play longer than two or three minutes."

"Yeah, but it probably kept you out of trouble!"

He grinned back at me. "True. At least I didn't lose my shirt at poker or have to dance with the old flapper."

"Flapper?"

"Yeah, I think Grazinsky arranged it. Some old lady who used to be a flapper twenty years ago. Grazinsky's idea of fun. She put on some kind of show, then danced with everybody. She even tried to sit in my lap but she kept bumping the phonograph, causing it to skip, so she gave up."

"Lucky you."

Keyes laughed again and rubbed his eyes, which I noticed were just a tinge red also and probably matched mine.

"So, Detective, getting back to the matter at hand, what's your next step?"

I shook my head. "I'm not sure, but something's just not right, Alan. It doesn't make sense. I've gone over every detail in my head, from the moment I stepped aboard."

"I know."

"Sorry, I've been dwelling on it when I should be concentrating on you." I ran my foot up the outside of his calf, my long legs allowing me to almost reach his crotch, unnoticed by anyone nearby since we were in a back booth next to the wall.

"You seem to be doing a pretty good job of managing both at the moment."

"I do what I can."

"And I appreciate that, Heath. As for dwelling on work, it's okay. It's your job, and I like listening to you sort things out. Besides, it's a working lunch, remember? We're on the payroll."

I smiled, glad Alan Keyes was no Riker. "You're right. Mind if I ask you something?"

He set down his cup and looked at me curiously. "Ask away, Detective."

"Be honest with me—have you ever heard any of the guys on the force talk about me or ask about me?"

"What do you mean?"

"Just in general, about my dating habits, or non-dating habits, or why I'm not married, the way I dress, that sort of thing."

"Oh." He looked down at his plate and moved the remains of his fish about with his fork.

"Well?"

"Sure, some. Everyone talks about everyone, you know that. It's human nature. I heard the talk about you before we'd even met."

"Really?"

He shrugged, still staring down at his plate. "Yeah. I was curious, of course, but I didn't put much stake in it, knowing how guys are."

"And when you finally met me at the Murdoch house, what then?"

"I didn't know what to think. You certainly didn't seem like, well, that way, but I liked what I saw and I guess I hoped." He looked up at me. "Why do you ask?"

"That undercover cop on the boat said he'd heard the guys talking about me."

"I see. Well, I wouldn't worry about it. They have no proof. It's just idle gossip."

"Vicious gossip, and I do worry about it. Maybe he and

my Aunt Verbina were right. Maybe I should get married and just have a fling on the side."

"Wowzer, that came out of left field, Detective."

"I'm sorry, Alan, I'm just thinking out loud, and I shouldn't be."

"No, you should be if it's on your mind. Is that really something you're thinking about?"

"You've thought about it. You told me yourself you thought about settling down, having kids, not wanting to die all alone," I countered.

"Yeah, and you're the one who told me we should live our lives to the fullest, that with a little luck maybe we can fight the world."

I stared at him hard, taking him all in. "Maybe we can fight the world, Alan. Damn it, I'm crazy about you," I said sincerely, lowering my voice to almost a whisper. "I don't want to get married, unless I can marry you."

He grinned at me. "If that's a proposal, I accept for better or worse."

I grinned back. "Good. Maybe in sixty or seventy years, it will be a different world and we can actually get married."

"I've always believed in long engagements, Detective."

I laughed. "Let's plan a trip again soon, just the two of us. Maybe to Chicago. Get a nice hotel room. Two beds, of course."

"That can be pushed together."

"And back again in the morning before the maid arrives."

"Of course."

"We'll do the town, be tourists, hang out at hidden rendezvous, maybe dance…"

"I'm not the best dancer."

"Doesn't matter. To me, you're Fred Astaire. I want to be

romantic with you to make up for our lost fishing trip, to make up for so many things."

"No arguments from me. I'm all in, just say when."

"Great!"

"And no murders or missing bodies. Just us this time, okay?"

"It's a deal."

"Just one thing—aren't we forgetting this is a working lunch?"

I sighed. "You distract me sometimes."

"Just sometimes?"

"All the time, but I do need to focus on business or I'll be out of a job, and then how can I take you to Chicago?"

"Fair enough. You were saying something didn't feel right."

"Yeah. Call me crazy, but something about this whole mess definitely bothers me. What's your take on it, Alan?"

"Me? I wasn't there, remember?"

"I know. I wish you had been. Maybe things would have turned out differently." I withdrew my foot from his leg as the busboy refilled our cups, and we spooned more ice into them.

"If I know you at all, I know you're blaming yourself for Slavinsky chucking himself overboard, if that is what happened."

I nodded slowly. "Yeah, you know me."

"But you can't do that. No one is to blame for that but himself."

"But I was assigned to watch him."

"You couldn't watch him all the time without either sharing a cabin with him or being shackled to him. You did the best you could under the circumstances."

I thought guiltily about the time in my cabin alone with

Riker when neither of us was paying any attention to Slavinsky. "I should have done more."

"Woulda, coulda, shoulda."

"Maybe. I still have a hard time believing he'd kill himself like that."

"But he left a note in his own handwriting, and he was being hounded by Ballentine for the money. Maybe he blew the money and figured he either takes his own life or lets Ballentine torture him."

"Perhaps. Neither of those are very appealing choices."

"No, but it makes sense. He booked the lake excursion thinking he could escape into Canada, but Ballentine joined him and he felt trapped. With no other way out, he chucked himself in."

"But if he really wanted to slip away, why not just slip away? Book passage under an assumed name. Using his own name doesn't seem very bright."

"True. I don't have an answer for that."

"Nor do I, yet."

"Maybe it never dawned on him that Ballentine was watching him so closely. Maybe he figured folks would think he was just taking a nice trip to Michigan and back."

"That's plausible."

"But not what you're thinking."

"It's like Ballentine is getting off too easy. Maybe Ballentine coerced Slavinsky into telling him where the money was, then he threw him overboard."

"So you think Ballentine did him in and faked the suicide or forced him to write the note before he killed him?"

"Again, it's a plausible theory. If he knew Slavinsky couldn't come up with the money, he would want to make an example of him. But a faked suicide wouldn't be Ballentine's

MO. He would want others to know what happened, to make an example of Slavinsky."

"But if Slavinsky had told him he had the money hidden somewhere, Ballentine would have no reason to keep him around, and going overboard in the middle of the lake seems like a tidy way to take care of him."

"I just can't see Ballentine successfully forcing Slavinsky into writing that suicide note, though. Why would Slavinsky do it? If he knew Ballentine was going to kill him, why write the note and basically let him off the hook, so to speak?"

Alan frowned as he sipped his coffee. "Maybe he threatened that sister you mentioned."

"That's actually a good thought, Keyes."

"Don't sound so surprised."

"Sorry, I didn't mean it that way. But that is a possibility I hadn't considered. Still, Ballentine would have nothing to gain making it look like a suicide."

"I don't know, sir. He's supposedly a respectable businessman now. He can't go around killing people that cross him, and you said yourself he suspected you. Maybe he figured you were a cop. Besides, I'm sure he'd find a way to make sure word got out on the street that Slavinsky was dead, and let folks think what they would. At the same time, the police couldn't pin anything on him."

I sat back and stared at him. "Impressive, Keyes—really impressive."

He grinned. "Thanks. I've been learning from you. But you still don't think it was Ballentine?"

"Call me crazy, but I just didn't get that feeling from him."

"But if Ballentine didn't kill him, Slavinsky had to have committed suicide, Heath. No one else on board had a motive from what you told me."

"There's George, I suppose. He's pretty loyal to Ballentine. Maybe he killed Slavinsky as a way of honoring Ballentine, but I don't really believe it."

"Hmmm."

"What?"

"Nothing, just wondering where Slavinsky hid all that money if he did still have it."

"That's what everyone wants to know. And if he didn't still have it, what did he blow it on? That's the twenty-five-thousand-dollar question, so to speak."

"Maybe he gambled it away, or maybe bad investments," Alan suggested.

"Maybe, but maybe he *did* hide it somewhere. If I was Ballentine, and Slavinsky did commit suicide, I'd want to find that money for sure before someone else did."

"All finished, gentlemen? Dessert?" The waiter had meandered over, looking sour as ever.

"Yes, all finished, and no dessert. Just the check, please."

"We have chocolate cake with mint ice cream."

"Tempting, but no."

He shrugged ever so slightly, his expression never changing. "As you wish." He motioned for the busboy, and together they cleared our table.

"I've got Riker watching Ballentine's house right now. He's to radio in if Ballentine leaves. While we wait for Mr. Charming to bring the bill, I think I'll check in and see if anything's happened yet, and also see what Fletch has turned up on that note. Excuse me, Alan."

"Don't forget your shoe, Cinderella."

I laughed and reached down to put my shoe back on. "Thanks, Prince. Say, got a nickel? I'm fresh out of change."

"Last of the big spenders, huh, Heath?" Alan tossed me a nickel and I winked at him as I caught it. I walked over to the phone booth near the door and dialed the number to the downtown station. "Hey, Kunkel, it's me, Barrington. Any word from Riker? No? Well, keep me posted if you hear anything. And get me Leslie Fletcher, please."

I heard Kunkel make the connection. "Fletcher."

"Hey Fletch, it's Heath. Any luck on that suicide note?"

"Heath. I tried you upstairs but they said you're out."

"Yeah, I'm at lunch at Schwimmer's."

"Nice place, great roast beef."

"I had the baked halibut."

"Fancy. Dining with anyone in particular?"

"Officer Keyes is with me. The chief cleared him to help me on the case."

"I see. I thought Riker was on this one with you."

"Riker's on stakeout over at Ballentine's place, but I also need Keyes's help with this one."

"Heath, you know what I'm going to say."

"Then don't say it, Fletch. I know what I'm doing."

He sighed. "I'd just be wasting my breath anyway, right? The note has three different prints on it: Riker's, yours, and Slavinsky's. The handwriting is definitely Slavinsky's, no doubt about it."

"Damn."

"Not what you wanted to hear?"

"I don't know. It certainly makes things more complicated."

"I would think it makes things simpler. You were assigned to watch Slavinsky, he threw himself overboard, end of story."

"Nice and neat."

"Exactly. I doubt anyone could have forced a guy like Slavinsky to write a suicide note and then throw him overboard," Fletch said.

"That actually was one of my theories. Stranger things

have happened, Fletch. Alan had a good theory on that note, too. Maybe he was right."

"What's his theory?"

"That someone forced Slavinsky to write that note under threat of harm to his sister and aunt."

"I suppose that's possible. You're the detective, not me, but from where I sit, it's a done deal. Suicide."

"Perhaps. Thanks for the info, Fletch. Let the desk know I won't be back for a while, will you? I think I want to have a look at Slavinsky's apartment."

"What for?"

"Just something Officer Keyes mentioned that got me to thinking."

"He seems to be saying a lot of things that get you to thinking."

"Yes, in more ways than one."

"You going to need a warrant?"

"Naw, no time for that. I'll just knock on the door, maybe have a chat with the building manager."

"Be careful, Heath. The chief is already pretty unhappy with you."

"Don't worry, I think we've made up for now. I'll check in later. Say hi to the wife."

"Will do. Bye, Heath."

I walked back to the booth and filled Alan in on what Fletch had told me.

"And knowing you, you're not willing to take that at face value."

"You do know me, Alan. Maybe it was suicide, but I want to make certain. You mentioned earlier about how Ballentine would want to find that money, and you might be on to something. Slavinsky's home address was listed in the dossier—let's go make a house call."

"You think the money may be there?"

"It's possible."

"But that doesn't make sense. He wouldn't escape to Canada and leave twenty-five grand hidden in his apartment."

"I agree. But maybe he was afraid Ballentine would follow him, and he left the money behind for an accomplice to bring up later."

"That would have to be a very trusted accomplice. Doesn't seem likely."

"Again, I agree, but the money wasn't on the boat or in Slavinsky's possessions. If he didn't blow through it, it has to be somewhere, and his apartment is as good a place as any to start looking. Perhaps he bought a valuable painting with the money and shipped it to Canada with the idea of selling it, or something like that. We may find a clue in his place, a receipt, something. It's worth looking, anyway."

"And if we find it what then? What would that prove? The money would have to be returned to Ballentine. I don't see as we'd have any legal hold on it, and it wouldn't prove or disprove how Slavinsky died."

"But maybe the money will lead us to something else that will prove what happened. Or perhaps we'll discover he really did blow the money on something. If that's the case, I'd feel better about the suicide angle. Either way, I have to investigate, at least. Maybe it will all be for naught, but I have to find out."

Keyes nodded. "Of course you do. Then to Slavinsky's place we go, sir."

"Thanks." I paid the bill, grabbed my hat, and headed out, Alan at my heels. "How did you get here?"

"I took the streetcar," he said.

"My car's at the station, let's go."

CHAPTER SIXTEEN

We walked back, heading north on Seventh to State Street, then one block west to the station, where my Buick was parked. The folder with Slavinsky's dossier was in the front passenger seat. "155 Water Street, the Golden Arms Apartments," I read aloud to Keyes, heading south to Wisconsin Avenue.

"The Golden Arms—sounds like a class joint."

"I'm sure." At Eighth and Wisconsin, I turned east and drove past the Schroeder and Randolph hotels, past Gimbels and Boston Store department stores, over the river to Water Street, where I turned again and headed south once more. It only took us about twenty minutes to get there, even with the afternoon traffic. The building was between Chicago and Erie Streets, in a run-down area near the warehouse district. I parked my car off Water, and we walked together to the corner.

"It should be on the west side of the street, Heath."

"Yes, that must be it. The Golden Arms looks a bit tarnished."

The building was cream city brick, but smoke from the nearby foundries had given it a gray cast. It was narrow and long, four stories high, with a stoop allowing access underneath to the basement units. Over the front door, a weathered wooden sign proclaimed the Golden Arms in what was apparently once gold paint. We went up the crumbling cement stairs and into the small, dark lobby. The front door had been propped open with a cinder block, probably because of the heat from yesterday, or maybe no one felt like opening and closing the door.

The lobby was dim and smelled old. I guessed the building was probably built in the early 1900s for immigrants. Past the dingy brass mailboxes was a long, narrow hallway with worn carpeting that had gray daisies on it that may have once been yellow. About midway down I could see the beginning of a staircase off to the right. I scanned the mailboxes for Slavinsky's name but didn't see it. "He's not listed that I can see."

"Are you sure this is the right place?" Alan said.

"It's the address listed in his file."

"Maybe he moved out."

"Maybe. Maybe he spent that money on some place a little more uptown. The manager is listed in 101. Let's just check before we go."

I rapped on the door, noticing the second "1" was missing a nail and swung back and forth with my knock. The sound of shuffling came from inside, and then the door opened a crack. A saggy gray eye appeared, looking us up and down below the chain, which kept the door from opening fully.

"Good day," I said.

Silence.

I pulled out my badge and ID and held it up to the eye. "I'm Detective Barrington with the Milwaukee Police, and this is Officer Keyes. We're looking for Gregor Slavinsky's apartment."

A pause, then the door shut and the chain came off before it opened enough for us to get a look at a stout, short old lady.

She had dull gray hair and grayer teeth. She wore no makeup and her face was pale, with folds of skin where there should have been cheeks. Her bosom was somewhere in the vicinity of her waist. She held a cigarette that sent up a trail of smoke curling about her head and mixing with the scent of cheap gardenia perfume.

"Good afternoon. ma'am. Does Gregor Slavinsky live in this building?"

"He did, but I heard he's dead," she said with about as much emotion as our waiter earlier.

"Yes, ma'am. I was on the boat when he went overboard early this morning. And you are?"

She took a drag on her cigarette before answering, dropping ash on her drab gray housecoat. Her feet were bare, her toenails painted red and chipped. "I'm Mrs. Price, the landlady."

"How do you do. So he does live here? His name wasn't on the mailboxes."

She blew a puff of smoke in my direction, which I did my best to wave away. "He moved in in February, but I ain't had time to put his name there. Ain't much point now."

"True," I replied, waving more smoke away.

"He was over two months behind on his rent. He finally paid up last week, but only because I threatened to call the cops on him."

"I did not know that."

"What do you want him for?"

"Police business."

"In trouble, was he? Not surprising."

"How did you hear that he was dead? It hasn't been in the papers yet that I'm aware of."

"Two fellas were here earlier today looking for him. They told me."

"Someone else was here today?"

"That's right, two of 'em. One said he was his brother, and the other a friend. They came together first thing. They're the ones that told me he was dead, like I said. The one didn't much look like a brother, though. Didn't look anything like Mr. Slavinsky."

"Are they still here?"

"No, they left a bit ago."

"What did they look like?"

More smoke, more ash. "Eh, the brother was dressed real nice, expensive. Kind of tall, but not as tall as you. He had short arms and legs, in his late forties or early fifties, I'd say. The other fellow was a big guy, real solid, and he had a small mustache, wide-set eyes, and a crooked nose, about the same age."

I glanced at Keyes. "That description sounds familiar. Did they go to Mr. Slavinsky's apartment? Did you let them in?"

"Yes and no. I told them I couldn't let them in but they were welcome to go up and knock on the door, though if he's really dead I'm sure he didn't answer."

"I'm sure not, Mrs. Price. Mind if we go up?"

"Suit yourself. Number 408 on the top floor, and we ain't got no elevator."

"The stairs are fine."

"I can't give you access to his apartment either, even if you are cops, unless you got a warrant."

"We'll just knock and take our chances."

"Free country. If he is dead, how am I going to get my money? Did he leave anything?"

"That I could not answer, Mrs. Price. I thought you said he paid his back rent a few days ago."

"He signed a year lease, and it's not up until the end of January. Twenty bucks a month."

"I'm sure you'll be able to re-rent it. There's a housing shortage, as you're certainly aware."

"Hmpfh, I'll have to get his stuff out of there and clean it up. I'll lose at least a month's rent if not more."

"If you wish, you may file a claim against his estate."

"Humph, his estate. He didn't have two nickels to rub together as far as I can tell, though that fellow that claimed to be his brother looked pretty well off, so maybe I will. And I'm going to sell off all of his stuff, too—so's I can get that apartment rented again to someone who pays rent on time."

"I would advise against disposing of his belongings, Mrs. Price, until family can be located and Mr. Slavinsky is officially declared deceased."

"His brother said he don't have any other family, so once he finished I was welcome to do what I wanted with Mr. Slavinsky's things."

"I would still advise against doing anything with his possessions for the time being, Mrs. Price. I'm told he has a sister and an aunt in California. I'll check in with you on our way out."

I tipped my hat, and we set off down the hall to the staircase. Mrs. Price was still watching us when we turned at the stairs, leaning against the door frame of her doorway, the glow of her cigarette a bright spot in the gloom. I nodded politely to her, and Keyes and I climbed the three flights of stairs to the fourth floor.

It was identical to the first floor. The light in the hall was dim, and the air smelled of mildew and stale smoke. I drew my gun as a precaution, but kept it low and at my side as we made our way toward the back of the building. From 403, we heard a radio playing too loudly, from 405 a man yelling and a baby crying. The door to 408 was ajar and had clearly been jimmied. Alan drew his gun as we pushed it open and stepped cautiously inside.

Either the place had been ransacked or Slavinsky was a very bad housekeeper. Drawers had been emptied, the Murphy bed had been pulled down, the mattress stripped and cut open, food dumped out of the refrigerator, sofa and chair cushions ripped apart, and the pictures taken off the wall. I nodded to a closed door next to the kitchenette, and Keyes made his way over there as I covered him.

He turned the knob slowly, then pushed it open, stepping aside and flattening himself against the wall, but nothing appeared. He reached in and pulled on a chain hanging from the ceiling, which cast a dull light over a small bathroom, empty except for layers of soap scum, grime, and a cockroach that quickly vanished into a crack in the wall. The door on the opposite wall was a closet, containing what few clothes Slavinsky didn't take with him on the boat, but nothing else.

It was a small studio apartment, the kitchenette and bathroom on the left wall, the closet and Murphy bed on the right wall, and two grimy windows in the far wall.

"Looks like Ballentine and George were looking for something."

"Why do you think it was Ballentine, sir?"

"He fits the description the landlady gave to a T, so does George, and it makes sense. They probably thought the same thing we did. We'll have to get the lab over here and dust for fingerprints. If nothing else, we can get Ballentine for breaking and entering and destroying private property."

I walked over to the phone next to the sofa and dialed the police station. Kangas answered. "It's Barrington, I'm over at Slavinsky's place—the door was jimmied, forced entry. Better send a black-and-white to 155 Water Street, the Golden Arms apartments, number 408, and I want someone from the lab here to dust for prints."

"Sure, Heath, I'm on it. Slow day here."

"Thanks. I'll wait until they get here. Any word from Riker yet?"

"Yeah, he said he's been at Ballentine's place for over an hour, but it doesn't look like he's even home."

"He must have gone straight from the boat to here. Tell Riker to stay put. Ballentine might be headed home next."

"Will do, Detective."

I hung up the phone and glanced around once more at the mess.

"Do you think they found anything, Heath?" Alan asked.

"Maybe."

"So, now what?"

"Now we have a look around while we wait for the lab guys and the black-and-white."

"A look around for what?"

"Maybe Ballentine missed something."

"We don't have a warrant, Heath."

"The door was open. We're just having a look around. No harm in that, is there?"

"I suppose not. Even if there was, you'd do it anyway."

I grinned at him and we put our guns away. He took the kitchenette and bathroom while I looked around the main room, trying not to disturb too much. I wasn't even sure what I was looking for as I searched through the debris. I flipped through cheesecake magazines, investigated the drawers and cabinets of the kitchenette, went through the pockets of the few clothes in his closet, and sifted through a small pile of underwear on the floor, but found nothing.

After about twenty minutes of searching, I called out to Alan. "Any luck, Keyes?"

He emerged from the bathroom. "Nope, nothing. I even looked in the toilet tank."

"Nothing out here, either. Slavinsky didn't leave much. He wasn't planning on returning, one way or another."

"Yeah, the bathroom's completely empty—not even a toothbrush. I can't believe that old lady gets twenty bucks a month for this dump."

"Before the war, she was probably getting ten. She's taking advantage of the housing shortage."

Keyes glanced about once more. "Why would Slavinsky live in a place like this?"

"According to his file, he was just released from prison in February. With no job per se and no references, this is probably all he could manage. Slavinsky was a sad sack with a whole lot of bad luck."

"Wowzer."

"Wowzer, indeed. I imagine as soon as he got out this last time, he looked up his old buddy Ballentine and worked up the investment deal to get him to fork over the money."

"Why would Ballentine ever have agreed to give Slavinsky that kind of money, even if it was a loan? It doesn't seem like a very good business decision."

"The two of them go back to bootlegging days in the twenties. If I had to guess, Slavinsky made this K-9 club idea sound like a sure thing, and Ballentine, maybe feeling he owed something to him out of loyalty to an old friend, agreed to loan him the money."

"That's quite a loan."

"It is, but to a guy like Ballentine, it's chump change."

"But even so, what was Slavinsky thinking, Heath? Surely he knew once Ballentine found out the whole thing was bogus, he'd want his money back and then some."

I shrugged. "My guess is the transaction took place,

and Slavinsky stalled, with the idea of taking the money and escaping to Canada, making a fresh start under an assumed name away from everyone and anyone Ballentine knows. But when Ballentine found out the building wasn't even for sale and that Slavinsky had booked the lake cruise, he decided to tag along just in case."

"That's quite a risk for Slavinsky to take. Ballentine isn't someone I would want to double-cross."

I shook my head. "Nor I." I glanced out the window and saw the black-and-white pull up. "Let's go, we're finished here. The boys just arrived downstairs."

"Yes, sir."

We climbed back over the debris and out into the hall. We met the two officers at the second floor landing, and I flashed them my ID.

"Afternoon, boys. It's apartment 408, top floor. The door frame's splintered, the lock forced, and the place has been ransacked. The lab is on the way over to dust for prints, so just wait in the hall until they get here. Tell them to ignore any prints of mine or Officer Keyes."

"Yes, sir."

"So what next?" Alan said when the two cops had continued their climb.

I didn't answer for a while, as I was completely perplexed and frankly out of ideas.

"I don't know, Alan. I honestly don't know." I felt defeated as we continued down the stairs to the first floor and rapped at the landlady's door once more.

Mrs. Price gazed out at us from yet another cloud of cigarette smoke. "Find anything?" she asked, her voice deep and raspy.

"No, he wasn't at home."

She laughed in a cackling sort of way. "The dead don't

usually answer doors, Detective. By the way, I saw two other policemen go up just now."

"Yes, that's right. And some men from the crime lab will be here shortly to take some pictures and whatnot."

"How come? He didn't die here, what's to take pictures of?"

"Someone broke into his apartment and ransacked it."

"Ransacked it? You mean they destroyed my furniture?"

"I'm afraid whoever did it made quite a mess, yes."

She took a long drag on her cigarette and blew out a cloud of smoke, coughing behind it. "Well, ain't that just great? That's gonna cost me more money."

"I'm afraid so."

"I knew Mr. Slavinsky was trouble. Sometimes you can just tell. I never shoulda rented to him."

"Well, he's dead now, Mrs. Price."

"Don't do me no good, but at least he didn't die here. Do you believe in ghosts, Detective?"

"Ghosts? I believe there are many things we're not fully aware of in this world, Mrs. Price, why?"

"I believe in them, but I ain't afraid of his ghost. Know why?"

"No, why?" I asked, curious to hear what she would say.

"Because he drowned. Ghosts can't travel over water, did you know that?"

"No, I did not."

"It's true, sure enough. Unless they have a vessel or something to travel in."

"Then perhaps he could come back in a boat."

She shook her head. "Ain't likely. My sister Vera's a spirit medium, she can tell you. If he drowned close to shore, he could inhabit a seagull. Vera tells me that's happened a few times, you know."

"I'll take your word for it, Mrs. Price. This world is enough for me to concentrate on. I'll leave the spirit world to the experts."

She bobbed her head up and down. "Vera's an expert, all right. She'll tell you anything you want to know and some things you don't want to know."

"I'm sure."

"So what am I supposed to do now, Detective?"

"Once the men from the crime lab are finished, they'll secure the apartment. I'm sorry, but you won't have access to it for a while. Once the judge has declared Mr. Slavinsky dead, you may inventory, remove, and store his belongings for thirty days. After that, you may dispose of anything unclaimed by any family members."

"I don't like the sound of that. How long will it take for the judge to declare him dead?"

"I'll need to conclude my case and submit evidence, but probably not more than a few days."

"Hmpf. I should hope not. I have bills to pay too, you know."

"I understand, Mrs. Price. By the way, did Mr. Slavinsky seem distraught to you? About the money he owed, his life?"

"Distraught? He didn't talk much to me because he owed me over two months' rent. But I wouldn't say he seemed distraught. He was a weaselly sort of man—small, nervous, very pale. Really not much of a man, and not much to him. He was only about five-six, and I think I outweighed him by over a hundred pounds. He had small hands, and feet, too. You know what they say about men like that."

"I can imagine, Mrs. Price. No need to tell me. Do you think he could have taken his own life?"

She shrugged and took another drag of her cigarette. "All kinds of people do all kinds of things, Detective. I'm just glad he didn't die here, all I'm saying. Spirits stay where they die, you know."

"So you've said."

"That's what Vera says. That's why I'm not afraid to get rid of his stuff. He can't harm me none, especially seeing as how he drowned."

"Yes, you mentioned that, too."

"Unless they have a vessel."

"Like a boat," I said.

"Yes, sir, but they can possess animals, birds, and people, too, you know." She looked hard at me, and then Keyes. "Animals, birds, or people that were there when they died, like you said you was."

"I assure you, Mrs. Price, we're not possessed."

"That's exactly what you would say if you was."

"And what would I say if I wasn't?" I asked.

She didn't have an answer for that, so she just puffed on her cigarette, dropping ash all about her, her saggy eyes wide.

"When did you last see Mr. Slavinsky?"

She scratched her head with her free hand and took another drag on the cigarette, which was almost done. "Tuesday last week, it was. I was watching for him because it's almost the end of May, and he still owed me for March and April. Of course he kept giving me sob stories, then he started avoiding me, like I said earlier, so I was watching for him."

"And you saw him last Tuesday."

"That's right. I remember because he came slinking in real quiet with some dandy and a woman, thinking he could slip right on by my door. He'd grown a beard and mustache, too— came in real red. Guess he thought it made him more manly looking, but it didn't help much. He looked like a leprechaun who'd lost his pot of gold." She laughed, dropping more ash.

"He wasn't alone?"

"No, but that didn't stop me. I flung open my door and said, 'Mr. Slavinsky, when are you gonna pay your rent? You'll be out on the street if I don't have my money by the first! Call the cops, I will,' I said to him."

"Seems more than fair."

"More than fair is right. Most landladies would have thrown him out after one month."

"So what did he do?"

"Oh, he acted all embarrassed and danced around a bit. He told the other two to go on up to his apartment, then he came over and acted all nice. He apologized and took out his wallet, gave me forty dollars cash on the spot. You coulda knocked me over with a feather. 'Course, like I said, he still owes me money, especially if the place is trashed. It's gonna take me a long time to get it rented again."

"I'm sure, Mrs. Price. What happened then?"

"Oh, he bid me good day and hightailed it down the hall and up the stairs. He didn't even wait for a receipt."

"Had you ever seen the man and woman before?"

She shook her head. "Nope, not that I can recall. Mr. Slavinsky had very few visitors."

"What did they look like? Was the man one of the men who were here earlier today?"

"Oh no. They asked me about them, too."

"They did?"

"Well, they asked if Mr. Slavinsky had any visitors recently, and that man and lady are the only ones I could think of."

"So what did they look like?"

"Oh, the man was nice looking, thin, very stylish, about forty years old, glasses. He wasn't much taller than Mr. Slavinsky, rather on the short side. He was carrying a big black leather case, too. Looked kind of heavy. He had a camera over his shoulder, which seemed kind of odd, and he fairly reeked of cigar smoke."

"I'm surprised you could smell that over your cigarettes," I stated somewhat sarcastically.

"Cigars smell much stronger, you know."

"I suppose so. What about the woman? What did she look like?"

Another puff on her cigarette as she thought, then finally, "Oh, she was probably in her thirties, maybe younger. She was slender, had on a dark coat and hat, red hair as I recall, nice enough looking, though she looked tired. At first I thought they was husband and wife."

"What made you change your mind?"

"When I confronted them, Mr. Slavinsky said, 'Take Miss Springer upstairs and wait for me.' Then the man said, 'Let's go, Trudy.' If they was husband and wife, she wouldn't be Miss Springer, would she?"

"No, that's a very good observation, Mrs. Price. Trudy Springer. Did you happen to catch the man's name?"

"No, they never said. I took a good look at her, though, to make sure she wasn't a lady of the evening, you know. I run a respectable house here. But she looked all right, I guess, a pretty girl, so I let it go. She looked a bit rough around the edges, though, if you know what I mean, and tired, like I said. She didn't move real fast."

"How very interesting. Did they stay upstairs long?"

"Not more than a couple of hours, then they left, alone. Mr. Slavinsky stayed upstairs."

"Did the man take the case with him?"

"Oh yes, definitely. And he still had that camera. What do you suppose they were up to?"

"I have no idea, but it's definitely curious. Well, Mrs. Price, thank you for your time. Someone from the police department will be in touch. We appreciate your cooperation."

"I'm going to file a claim, you know."

I tipped my hat. "You do that, Mrs. Price. Good day."

CHAPTER SEVENTEEN

W e walked out onto the stoop and down the steps, glad to be back in the fresh air. At the corner, I turned to Keyes. "Things have gotten interesting again."

"The man and woman?"

"Yes, indeed. And the beard and mustache."

"I get the couple being interesting, but why the facial hair?"

"Just curious he would choose to grow it out now. In every photo I've ever seen of him, he's always been clean-shaven."

"Maybe he was trying to disguise his appearance."

"By growing a beard and mustache, yes, or perhaps by shaving it off."

"Huh?"

"Nothing, just a thought I had. Right now I'm more interested in the man and woman. There's a phone booth over there, let's see if we can get lucky."

We crossed Water Street to a phone booth on the opposite corner, and I flipped through the phone book to the Springers. "Hmmm, there's a listing for a T. Springer at 812 Knapp Street, Liberty 5-52289."

"I've got a nickel if you want to call."

"Knapp Street's not that far. Let's pay a visit instead. I don't want to scare her off if she happens to be home."

"Fair enough. Let's go."

We walked briskly back to my car and headed north. The address was between Cass and Marshall, about ten minutes from where we were. We pulled up to the three-story red brick building and parked beneath an old elm tree.

The directory in the outer lobby listed T. Springer and A. Lamb in apartment 2B. We rang and waited.

A woman's voice answered. "Yes?"

I looked at Keyes, then ad-libbed, "Heath Barrington here. I'm looking for Trudy."

"She's not here."

"May I leave something for her?"

A pause, then the door buzzed and we were in. We climbed the stairs to the second floor, where we knocked on the door of 2B.

A woman who appeared to be in her late twenties, possibly early thirties answered. She was attractive enough, bleach blond, dark roots, still had her figure, fairly tall, about five-nine. She wore a low-cut green dress with a yellow sash about her waist. Her feet were bare, her toenails the same color of pink bubblegum as her fingernails.

"Good afternoon, miss. We're looking for a Miss Trudy Springer."

She looked us up and down. "So you said. You didn't say you were cops, though. I figured you were one of her gentleman friends. What's this about? You said you had something you wanted to leave for her?"

I shook my head. "Sorry, that wasn't true, but I wasn't sure you'd let us in otherwise. I'm Detective Barrington, this is Officer Keyes."

"Cops at our door are never good, though you're not the first and you surely won't be the last. Trudy lives here, but she's not home right now. Why are you looking for her?"

"We just want to ask her some questions, that's all."

"She in some kind of trouble?" she asked, still looking us up and down.

"Not that we're aware of. I just want to talk to her about some people she may know. Are you a friend of hers?"

"We're roommates. I'm Allison Lamb."

Do you know where she is, Miss Lamb?"

She shook her head. "Nope. She was all excited about a job out of town is all I know. She packed a bag and left yesterday."

"Job?"

"She's a model and an actress, at least when she can land something. Lately, it's been few and far between. So what's this all about, Detective? Are you sure Trudy isn't in some kind of trouble? A problem with one of her gentlemen?"

"She may have information regarding a case we're working on. When is she expected back?"

She laughed a bit harshly. "I never know with Trudy. She doesn't tell me much, and I don't think she knows herself. She disappears for days sometimes, even weeks. When she comes back, she either can't remember where she was or doesn't want to tell me."

"Does she have any family?"

"None to speak of that I know, anyway. She's from a small town up north, but she's been on her own here since she was fifteen. Her parents are dead, I think."

"Fifteen is awfully young to be on your own."

"Trudy's tougher than she looks, Detective, and so am I. A girl figures out ways to survive."

"I'm sure."

"Look, whatever you think she did, I don't know anything about it, okay? She lives her life, I live mine." I heard the door across the hall open behind me. "Good afternoon, Mrs.

McDermott," Miss Lamb said rather loudly over my shoulder. I heard the door close again. "Busybody. She watches us like a hawk. She's called the police on us a few times, too. If you have more questions, you might as well come in where we can talk in private. I have to get ready for work soon anyway."

"Thanks." We stepped inside, removing our hats, and glanced about. The apartment was small but clean and tidy, all the upholstery covered in chintz. "We won't take up much of your time, but I do have a few more questions for you, if you don't mind."

"Fine by me, I suppose. It's your nickel. At least you two are nice enough to look at. May I take your hats?"

"We're fine, thank you."

"Might as well have a seat, then. I spend too much time on my feet at work to be standing around at home. Can I get either of you a cigarette?"

"Ah, no thank you, we don't smoke."

"I'm trying to quit myself. How about some coffee? I just made a fresh pot."

"None for me, thanks. Keyes?"

"No thank you, ma'am."

"Suit yourself. We don't keep booze in the house because of Trudy." She sat down on the sofa, crossing her legs, and I positioned myself next to her. Alan took the wing chair by the window and readied himself to take notes.

"Because of Miss Springer?"

"Yes, she likes the bottle. She goes on and off the wagon."

"I see. You mentioned earlier that she has gentlemen friends, visitors."

"She does sometimes. What of it?"

"Just curious. I don't imagine acting pays the rent much, and it doesn't sound like she has any steady job. Do you have gentleman callers, too?"

"What are you implying?"

"Just an observation, Miss Lamb."

She shrugged. "Trudy does some odd jobs here and there when she's sober, and yes, she has her gentleman callers. So do I sometimes, though Trudy entertains more than I do. What's wrong with that?"

"Nothing, on the surface."

"I just mean they take us out to dinner and buy us stuff sometimes, you know. It's all legit, nothing illegal."

"Of course."

"Trudy doesn't have any other regular job, but I'm a waitress. I work nights. That is, when I don't have an acting job. I act when I can, and I do modeling on the side, mostly lingerie. Would you like to see my portfolio?" She raised her left brow and looked at me rather coyly.

"Uh, thanks, maybe another time," I said.

"Suit yourself. You're an odd fellow. Anyway, Lamb's my stage name. I was born Allison Labronski, but I thought Allison Lamb had a nicer ring to it."

"It does," I agreed. "And all those gentlemen can't resist a pretty little lamb."

"You have a way of saying things that don't sound very nice sometimes, Detective. I work hard at the diner. Sometimes I meet men that want to treat me to things, so does Trudy. They like to take care of us, and we let them."

"In exchange for a little female company."

"That doesn't sound very nice when you say it, either. What kind of a case are you working on, anyway?"

"I'm afraid that's classified. So you mentioned Miss Springer left early yesterday afternoon for an out-of-town job?"

"That's right. Some kind of acting job or an audition. I'm not really sure, but I know it paid pretty well. That's Trudy's acting portfolio there on the coffee table. She leaves it out so people can see it. I keep mine in the closet, but if you change your mind, I can get it easily enough, or perhaps you would prefer a live demonstration."

I felt myself blush. "I'm sure your portfolio is exceptional Miss Lamb, but we're in a bit of a hurry at the moment."

"Just trying to be friendly."

"Really not necessary, but thank you." I picked up Trudy's scrapbook and leafed through it, looking at various newspaper clippings of shows and plays, pictures of her in assorted poses and outfits, headshots and glamour shots. Most looked several years old. One of the photos was in color, and I found her red hair striking, her deep blue eyes soulful. I felt as if I'd known her, or perhaps I saw her in one of her plays. "It's quite the portfolio."

"Yes, though most of it's pretty old. Her one starring role was over five years ago. Since then, she's had more bit parts than Carter's got liver pills."

"That must be quite frustrating for her."

"I suppose so. It's been the same with me, but I'm satisfied to waitress and take the occasional acting or modeling job at this point. We both came here young, hoping to break into the theater, move on to bigger shows in Chicago and eventually New York. Now, fifteen years later, we're still here where we started. Trudy, she still wants the glitz, the glamour, the adoration. I mean we all do, of course, but she really wants it, poor thing."

"Why 'poor thing'?"

"As I mentioned before, Trudy likes the bottle a little too much, if I can be frank. That's why we don't keep alcohol in the apartment. She can't resist it. She's taken to pills, too—pills to put her to sleep, pills to wake her up, pills to calm her down, pills to get her moving. When she's sober and off the pills, she's great, but she's a real mess when she's on them. She can be really, really happy, or really, really sad, sometimes in the same hour. I never know what to expect from her."

"That must be difficult for you both."

She nodded. "It can be. One of her gentleman friends was a doctor. He got her on the pills, the jerk. She's best when she's off them, you know? When she's got an acting job, I mean, and she's sober. She's really quite a good actress, and she lives for it. But the rejections are tough, and in a small place like Milwaukee there aren't that many opportunities, know what I mean?"

"Yes, I think I do."

"We've both done some work in Chicago, and Trudy still talks about moving to New York, but I don't think she ever really will. Of course, she's two years older than me, you know. And she looks older, too. It's the booze and the pills."

"They can take their toll on a person."

"You're telling me. They've really aged her even in the short time I've known her. She doesn't get as many gentleman callers these days, and when she does, they're anything but gentlemen."

"That's unfortunate. So she's never made it big with her acting?"

?. "Not big, big. But Trudy had her one time in the spotlight, one big starring role. She played Juliet in *Romeo and Juliet*. That's the program there, way back in forty-two during the war. Her leading man was only seventeen. Everyone else had been drafted or enlisted."

I picked up the yellowed program that had been loosely placed in a sleeve of the scrapbook and stared at the picture of Miss Springer on the cover. "She certainly was quite an attractive woman then."

Miss Lamb looked down at it. "Yes, that was taken over

existed?

five years ago, like I said. She was twenty-five then, though she tells people she was twenty."

"Typical, I suppose."

"The years really haven't been kind to Trudy. I feel kind of sorry for her, you know? I mean, she's my friend and all, but I feel sorry for her even though we're not all that close."

"She never married?"

Miss Lamb shook her head. "No, Trudy's not the marrying kind. She's had more than a few men, though, bless her heart, including a few married ones—her gentleman callers, as I mentioned."

"Yes, you did mention that."

"Not that there's anything wrong with that."

"Actually there is, if these gentlemen are paying for the pleasure of her company or yours, Miss Lamb."

She laughed. "A girl's got to do what a girl's got to do, Detective. She can go to sleep with her dignity and her virtue, or she can go to sleep with a man and wake up with money to pay the rent. What's the difference if he gives her a diamond bracelet or cash the next morning? Or if he takes her out to a nice dinner the night before in anticipation? Frankly, I don't see the harm in it, and I don't see that it makes a difference."

"You make a good point, but I don't write the law. I only enforce it."

"The law—fat lot of good that does a working girl. I'm not saying Trudy does or doesn't, and I'm not saying I do or don't, but I don't judge people, and I don't like those that do. What goes on between two consenting adults is fine by me."

"To be honest, I agree with you. So these gentleman callers help you pay the rent."

"What if they do? You figure it out. A place like this would be hard to come by on a waitress's tips and the occasional acting job. We don't charge for our company, Detective, but we don't say no to presents, either."

"Interesting."

"I was married once, you know."

"Oh? Are you a widow?" I asked, somewhat surprised.

She laughed again. "No, not a war widow, though there's plenty of those around. I'm a divorceé."

"How interesting."

"He was a louse. My ex, I mean, but I found out too late. We divorced three years ago, and I moved in here with Trudy. At least neither one of us never had kids."

"Something to be thankful for, I suppose. Where exactly do you and Miss Springer meet your gentlemen callers?"

"Here and there. Sometimes at the diner, sometimes Albert introduces us to friends of his. We don't stand on street corners, if that's what you're implying, Detective. Like I said, we don't charge for the pleasure of our company. Trudy and I aren't those kinds of girls. I waitress full-time and Trudy does odd jobs when she can get them."

"Waitressing is hard work, indeed."

"You don't know the half of it, Detective. Long hours, rude customers, lousy pay. It's a killer on the back and feet."

"So who is this Albert you mentioned?"

"Just a fella we know. He does makeup for the theaters sometimes."

"And he introduces you to men and takes part of their generosity as payment."

She shook her head. "Again, you say things and they don't sound nice."

"I don't know how else to say it, but I'll take that as a yes." I flipped through the program, looking at scene descriptions, credits of other cast members, and bios. "I see you were in

Romeo and Juliet, too, Miss Lamb. 'Allison Lamb, young maiden, ensemble.'"

"That's right, I had a non-speaking role. That was the first show Trudy and I did together. And Albert did the makeup. He stopped by to see Trudy a couple weeks ago."

"What's Albert's full name?"

"Albert Baines. His name's listed there." She pointed to a small column on the right of the page in the program.

"Costumes by Brenda Trotier Snyder, makeup by Albert Baines," I read aloud.

"Yes, Brenda and Albert were quite the pair. Brenda did a lot of the costumes for the shows back then. She could make a ball gown out of a gunnysack. She made a lot of the jewelry, too. I heard she got married and retired a few years back, though, lucky girl."

"What's the makeup man like?"

"Albert? He's a womanizer, a dog, always dating some young starlet. He loves them and leaves them."

"Sounds like quite a rogue."

"Yes. A real whiz when it comes to makeup, though. He once made an eighteen-year-old pimple-faced, freckled kid look just like Abraham Lincoln, beard and all. I mean, you would swear it was old Abe himself."

"Quite a talent."

"We all thought he'd end up on Broadway, but he never seemed to get the big break, either."

"Show business is tough."

"You're telling me. And Albert's got real ability when he's not wheeling and dealing or getting in trouble."

"What kind of trouble?"

"Money trouble, usually. Girl trouble always."

"Mr. Baines was short on cash?"

Allison laughed again. "He works in the theater, Detective. Very few theater people have what you would call a lot of money. He's sharing a one-bedroom apartment with two other fellows just to make ends meet. Albert's a schemer, always working up some get-rich-quick scheme, but never quite working out."

"On the up-and-up?"

She shook her head. "Not always. He has had a few scrapes with the law, if you must know. He did some time in jail a year or so ago to no one's surprise."

"But you and Miss Springer both know him fairly well, it sounds like."

"We met him at the theater, of course, years ago. He's all right. He knows a lot of wealthy men. Wealthy, lonely men that want some company sometimes, and he introduces us. Not just us, but girls in the shows that need an occasional helping hand, if you know what I mean. Some of the boys, too, if that's what they want."

"I see. How nice of him to help them out," I said sarcastically. "Is that what he wanted to see Miss Springer about?"

She shook her head again. "Not this time. He's the one that got her the job or audition or whatever it is this weekend. He's back to doing makeup now that he's out of the slammer, and he acts occasionally, both here and in Chicago, so he has lots of connections."

"You mentioned he stopped by to see her a couple weeks ago. And he got her this job she's on now?"

"Yeah, it was funny. Last time either one of us saw him was at the Grand downtown about two months ago on a show that went nowhere but down. Trudy and I both had bit parts in it, and Albert did the hair and makeup. We closed after two nights, no fault of our own, I must say, and we went our separate ways. Then about two or three weeks ago, he stopped by to see Trudy."

"Were you home at the time?"

"Yes, but I don't know much more about it than what I just told you. They were kind of secretive about it all, but that's the way theater people are."

"What do you mean?"

"If someone has an angle on a good role, an audition or a reading, they don't want anyone else horning in on it. I'm sure she figured if I heard about the role, I'd want to try out for it, too. Or I'd say something to someone who wanted to audition for it, see?"

"Yes, I see. She wanted to keep the competition to a minimum."

"I don't blame her. I'd do the same thing, we all do. Anyway, when she left yesterday, she had packed a bag and said she'd probably see me in a few days. I'm curious to know what kind of part she was up for. Trudy likes her booze and her pills, and she can be difficult, but Albert knows that. He never even asked me if I'd be interested."

"Perhaps you didn't fit the physical characteristics, Miss Lamb."

She shrugged. "Maybe so."

"So you don't know what the part was or where she went?"

"No, sorry, I don't. But obviously it's an out-of-town audition, seeing as how she packed a bag and all. She said she'd be back in a few days, but who knows with her? She may show up in a few days or she may be gone weeks."

"Do you know if Mr. Baines was with her?"

"Yes, he picked her up. I know they were headed to Chicago on the train, but from what little I heard, that wasn't their final destination."

I looked over at Keyes, but he was scribbling away taking notes. "How would you describe Mr. Baines, physically, Miss Lamb?"

"Albert? Oh, he's about five-eight, dark, kind of wavy hair, glasses, clean shaven. Nice enough looking for a shorter fellow, though don't tell him I said that. He's conceited enough as it is."

"How old?"

She laughed. "Early fifties, I think, though age isn't discussed much in the theater."

"And have you ever heard the name Gregor Slavinsky?"

She furrowed her brow. "That's an interesting name, but it doesn't ring a bell. Why?"

"Just curious. I was wondering if he was one of her gentleman callers."

"Could be. I don't always remember their names, and neither does Trudy."

"Fascinating. Do you happen to know where Mr. Baines lives?"

"Him and those two other fellas got a flat on Wisconsin in the Arcadia building, near the Alhambra Theater. I've been to a party or two there. Why do you ask?"

"No reason. Thank you for your time, Miss Lamb. We won't detain you any longer. If you hear from Miss Springer, will you have her give me a call? Here's my card."

She took it, glanced at it, then set it on the table next to her. "Sure thing, though I'm not sure when she'll show up again. You're sure she's not in any trouble, though?"

"Not that I'm aware of, Miss Lamb."

"That's good. Trudy's a mess sometimes, but she's not a bad person, really."

"I'm sure not. Thank you again for letting us in and speaking to us."

"No skin off my nose, Detective. I'm always happy to entertain handsome men."

"Uh, thank you."

"Are you boys married?"

I glanced over at Keyes, but he still had his nose in his notebook.

"No, ma'am," I replied.

"So, no wives waiting at home? You know what they say about us divorcées and working girls."

I felt my face flush. "I'm sure it's all true, Miss Lamb."

"I could be late for work." She smiled at me and then over at Keyes and uncrossed her legs.

"But I can't. Let's go, Keyes."

"Yes, sir."

We stood up and walked to the door, Miss Lamb following us.

"I'm home most mornings and early afternoons, or you can visit me at the diner—Dick's on Fourth. We're up and open all night. I pour a hot, steaming cup of coffee that will curl your toes, extra sugar. And two handsome men like you wouldn't even have to tip."

"We'll keep that in mind, Miss Lamb."

"Please do."

I smiled, put my hat back on, and nodded. "Good day."

"See you in the funny papers, Detective, Officer."

I opened the door and Keyes and I walked out. Mrs. McDermott peered at us from her door across the hall, open just a crack. I nodded to her, too, and we went down the hall toward the stairs to the first floor and out into the afternoon sunlight, where we stopped beneath the large elm tree to catch our breath.

"So what do you think?" I asked, turning to him.

"I think Miss Lamb wants to do more than pour us a cup of hot coffee, sir."

I laughed. "I can't say I blame her, Officer, at least not where you're concerned. But what do you think about Miss Springer?"

"On that I'm confused, sir. Trudy Springer and some gentleman who may have been this Albert Baines paid a visit to Mr. Slavinsky's apartment, and she is an actress. And she left yesterday with this Albert Baines. What's it all mean?"

"What do you think it means?"

"I don't know. Maybe Slavinsky was dating her?"

"He was doing something to her, but I don't think they were dating."

"It did cross my mind that Slavinsky may have paid for her services, so to speak, and this Mr. Baines was indeed her, uh, manager."

"That crossed my mind, too, which is why I pressed Miss Lamb about the gentleman callers. It certainly sounds like Miss Springer could be persuaded to spend an hour or two with Gregor Slavinksy for a modest sum, and he clearly had the money. But I think there was more to it than paid bedroom services. Did you notice Albert Baines's name?"

"What about it?"

"It's similar to Alex Bains Whitaker, the fellow on the boat with his aunt."

"You're right, Heath. Curious."

"Yes, that's what I thought, too. And the description Mrs. Price gave of the man with Miss Springer, and Miss Lamb's description of Mr. Baines are similar."

"Gee willikers! You mean you think Albert Baines and Mr. Whitaker are the same person?"

"That's my working hypothesis at the moment, yes."

"But you said Slavinsky and Whitaker hadn't met before the boat."

"That's what I was made to believe, yes. I think we need to do a little more investigating on Mr. Whitaker and his aunt."

"How do we find them?" Alan asked. "They could be anywhere by now."

"He told me they were going to spend the night at the Water's Edge Motel down near the docks."

"Do you think that was the truth?"

"They aren't aware we suspect them of anything, so I don't think they'd be in a rush to get out of town. The motel's a good place to start, anyway. They didn't go to Slavinsky's, and they aren't here, so chances are they decided to stay over at the motel and sort things out. If they're not there, we'll check Albert Baines's apartment, though I doubt they'd go there with two roommates. I imagine when the boat was forced to return to Milwaukee, it must have thrown their plans for a loop."

"Makes sense to me. Let's go."

CHAPTER EIGHTEEN

We climbed back into my Buick, and I headed the car south and east toward the docks. As I drove, I glanced over at Keyes, who seemed lost in thought.

"What's on your mind, Alan?"

"Hmmm? Oh, just trying to sort this all out."

"And?"

"Well, if this Albert Baines really was Mr. Whitaker, Miss Springer was playing Mrs. Woodfork."

"That's my thought, too. She was hired by Baines to play the part."

"So it makes sense that Baines knew Slavinsky and knew where the money was, so he and Miss Springer bumped him off," Alan stated.

"That's a theory. But why bother having her dress up like an old lady?"

"Because Slavinsky knew what Miss Springer looked like, sir. Remember, she and Baines came to his apartment."

"So?"

"So Baines needed someone on board to help him. Maybe slip a mickey into Slavinsky's drink and help him hoist Slavinsky's body overboard. He hired Trudy to be undercover."

"It's a good possibility, Keyes. But why was Baines even

aboard? Did Slavinsky invite him? If so, why? And if he just showed up uninvited with his 'aunt,' wouldn't that make Slavinsky suspicious? And why would they pretend not to know each other? And why did Baines and Miss Springer go with Slavinsky back to his apartment?"

Keyes frowned. "All good questions."

I sighed. "Also, what about the suicide note? If Baines and Miss Springer did kill Slavinsky, how did they get him to write the suicide note? Did they know about his sister and aunt? So many good questions and so few answers."

"You'll find them."

"Thanks, Alan. *We'll* find them. Together."

He looked over at me and smiled, then turned back to the window. We rode a ways in silence, both of us mulling over the unanswered questions. A few blocks from our destination, Alan looked over at me. "Heath, I just had another thought."

"I'm all ears."

"What if Miss Springer was actually impersonating Gregor Slavinsky?"

"Huh?"

"Well, I remember you saying he had grown a beard and mustache, which he had never done before. What if that was actually Miss Springer and Slavinsky was the old lady?"

"Interesting, Keyes, but to what purpose?"

"Hmmm, I'm not sure about that part yet. Maybe so Slavinsky could slip away while Ballentine was watching Springer, who was dressed as Slavinsky."

"Doesn't seem logical, Alan. I think Ballentine would have seen through that, as he knew Slavinsky pretty well. Besides, remember, Mrs. Price saw Slavinsky with the facial hair, and he was with Miss Springer and Baines at the time."

"Oh. Yeah, you're right."

"Keep thinking, though, Alan. I'm open to any and all ideas."

"Yes, sir."

I slowed my car as I turned onto Howell Avenue. The Water's Edge Motel was not far from Humboldt Park, across the street and on the corner. The motel was located near the pier, a convenient place to spend the night for people who were catching early-morning ferries or boats across the lake.

The motel was small, but nice enough looking. I parked on the street just up the block, not wanting Baines or Miss Springer to see me should they happen to look out. "Let's go around to the rear and come up the side to the office."

"I'll follow you, sir."

I nodded. It was a good feeling to have someone with me I could trust.

The office was to the side, on the short end of an L shape. A bell jingled as we entered. We closed the door behind us, listening to it jingle again. A stout older man appeared from the back, a well-chewed toothpick dangling from his lips and suspenders holding up his baggy trousers. His necktie was loose around his neck, his shirt collar unbuttoned.

"Hello, there. How can I help you gentlemen?" He looked at Alan's uniform as he added, "Anything wrong?"

"Perhaps, perhaps not, sir. I'm Detective Barrington, Milwaukee Police, this is Officer Keyes. And you are?"

"Nelson, Frank Nelson. I'm the owner here. I run a clean place, Detective. None of that rooms-by-the-hour stuff here. I rent by the day or week only. I've never had any trouble, and I don't want any now."

"I'm sure you have a very upstanding establishment, Mr. Nelson. We're not here to investigate you or your motel. We're looking for a fellow by the name of Baines, or perhaps

Whitaker, possibly with an elderly woman named Mrs. Woodfork."

He took the toothpick out of his mouth and tossed it in a can behind him. "Funny. You're the second person today came looking for them, Detective. The man's brother and a friend got here about half an hour ago."

Keyes and I looked at each other. "Don't tell me, Mr. Nelson—the brother was nicely dressed, kind of tall, short arms and legs, in his late forties or early fifties. The other fellow was a big, solid guy about the same age with a small mustache, wide-set eyes, and a crooked nose."

"That's them all right. You know 'em?"

"We're acquainted. Are they still here?"

He shook his head. "Not sure. They said they were going to surprise Mr. Whitaker and his aunt. Odd fellows, those two. They didn't seem totally on the up-and-up."

"I'd say that was an astute observation, Mr. Nelson. So, Mr. Whitaker and his aunt are staying here then?"

"Yes, sir. They checked in earlier today. Came in a taxicab. Not too many folks do that, at least not here."

"No?"

"Nope. Most folks drive, some come by bus. The war nearly killed the place—I'd be lucky to rent a room a week. Even now it's quiet."

"It will pick up again, I'm sure, Mr. Nelson."

"I hope so. I'd like to retire, get out of this weather, do some fishing."

"Yes, of course. Now, about Mr. Whitaker and his aunt…"

He scratched his crotch. "Right. They said they're catching the train to Michigan tomorrow. They said somebody killed himself on a boat they were on the other day, so that's why they had to return to port. Mr. Whitaker seemed pretty upset about it all. Of course you, being the police, probably know all about that."

"Yes, we're aware of the death on the boat. What room are Mr. Whitaker and Mrs. Woodfork in?"

"A12, just down the way and to the left. They're not in any trouble, are they?"

"They may be in trouble, they may be in danger, or they may be dangerous. I'm not sure yet."

"Oh, dear." He took another toothpick from his front shirt pocket and stuck it in his mouth. "They seem like such nice folks, real quiet. Mrs. Woodfork even tipped me fifty cents for carrying her bags, when most people only give me a quarter, if anything. She seemed such a sweet woman, but a bit frail and nervous. A widow, you know, real recent."

"Appearances can be deceiving, Mr. Nelson."

"I suppose you're right, but I can't imagine how either of them could be dangerous, and I certainly hope they're not in danger."

"That remains to be seen. Thanks for your help, sir. Please stay in here until we check back with you."

"Yes, Detective, Officer."

Keyes and I exited the office, the bell on the door jingling again, and we made our way quietly down the walk and to the left, where a walkway separated the short part of the L from the long part. A12 was near the end, and the door was ajar and had clearly been jimmied, just like at Slavinsky's. Keyes and I approached cautiously, drawing our guns. I hoped no other guests were about and being nosy. The last thing I needed was some lady poking her head out of a door to see what was going on and getting herself accidentally shot.

We almost tiptoed the last few steps, and I pushed on the jimmied door, which thankfully swung open silently. I peered around the corner and looked in, Keyes behind me. The room had been searched like Slavinsky's apartment, with drawers pulled out, mattresses turned over, and everything scattered about. Over by the far bed two men had their backs to us, apparently literally ripping apart the two suitcases on the stands down to the lining and making enough noise to allow us to enter the room completely unheard.

"Freeze! Police!" I said loudly. Fortunately, they did.

"Hands up. We have two revolvers aimed right at you."

They raised their hands, still facing the wall.

"Turn around, slowly." It was definitely Ballentine and George, the overhead light shining on their faces.

"Hey, Mr. Benson. What are you doing here?" George called out, surprise in his voice.

"Shut up, George. He's a cop, remember? A dick?"

"Oh yeah, right. I forgot," he said, sounding disappointed.

"A police detective, actually, Ballentine. What are you two doing in Whitaker's motel room, as if I didn't know."

"If you know, why ask?"

"You're looking for that twenty-five grand of Gregor Slavinsky's."

"Wrong, Detective. I'm looking for that twenty-five grand that belongs to me."

"And you tore apart Slavinsky's apartment earlier today looking for it there, too."

"I ain't admitting anything to you."

"You don't have to. I'm sure your prints are all over everything in his apartment. The boys from the lab are going over it right now, and I'll get them over here shortly. I take it you haven't found what you're looking for yet, or you wouldn't still be here."

"My, you are a bright one."

"And what you're doing is illegal, Mr. Ballentine.

Trespassing, destroying private property, breaking and entering, among other things."

"So arrest me."

"Don't think I won't. You should have made sure you had your money back before you killed Slavinsky." I was grasping in the dark, but I figured it was worth a shot.

He and George laughed. "I didn't kill the louse, and neither did George. He's worthless to us dead. That cash was a loan, and we want it back."

"I'm sure you do, and I want to know who killed him."

"He killed himself, Detective, remember? He even left a note."

"Yes, but my instincts tell me otherwise."

"Do they now? Look, my hands are getting tired. Are you going to arrest me or not?"

"Keep your gun on them, Keyes," I said as I moved slowly toward Ballentine and frisked him. I found a small revolver tucked in his sock garter. I frisked George next, finding a revolver, brass knuckles, and a switchblade.

"Impressive, George."

"Thanks, Mr. Benson. I'm gonna need those back, though."

"I see you ripped open Whitaker's suitcase," I stated, ignoring George's comment.

"I ain't admitting nothing."

"So, you are admitting something, then," I said.

"What are you talking about?" Ballentine asked.

"You used a double negative, which makes a positive."

"What the hell are you on about? You ain't making no sense." Ballentine looked confused.

"Ah yes, so I'm glad you agree I'm making some sense, anyway."

They both stood there looking at me blankly, so I

continued. "Your search of Slavinsky's place and this room didn't turn anything up, then?"

Silence from both of them.

"Like I said, gentlemen—and I use that term loosely—I can prove you were there, and you've obviously had a look about here and were caught red-handed, so you might as well tell me."

"Eh, there ain't much to tell, Detective," Ballentine said at last. "Just a lot of cockroaches at Slavinsky's, and a dead body in the bathtub here, in there." Ballentine jerked his head toward a door next to the bed.

"What?!"

Ballentine shrugged nonchalantly. "Oh yeah, I forgot to mention that. But we had nothing to do with it. If you check our guns, you'll see they haven't been fired recently, and the body in there was definitely shot through the head."

"Keep them covered while I take a look, Keyes." I went toward the partially open door next to the far bed and pushed it with my foot.

"The light is a pull chain, Detective."

"Thanks." I gave it a tug, bathing the small room in a dusty light. The man in the tub was face up, with a neat bullet hole in his right temple, a river of blood down his face, his wire glasses askew. He was dressed in a simple brown suit with a white carnation in his lapel. It was Mr. Whitaker, Alex Bains Whitaker, or Albert Baines, as the case may be. I shuddered involuntarily, then pulled the chain again and returned to the living room.

"You know who that is?" I said.

"Sure, don't you?"

"Mr. Whitaker, from the boat."

"Yup, I recognized him, too. Makes sense, since this is his room."

"And you're telling me he was dead when you got here?"

"That's right, Detective. When we got here, the door was locked. George managed to open it with just a little gentle persuasion. Nothing looked out of place or out of the ordinary. The shades were drawn and it was kind of dark, but the beds was made, everything was normal. Then George checked the bathroom, and we found him."

"And you didn't think to call the police?"

George laughed. "Now why would we go and do that?"

Ballentine nodded in agreement. "Exactly, George. Whitaker was already dead, and we needed to find our money. Calling the police wouldn't have helped him any, and it certainly wouldn't have helped us, now would it?"

"And why did you two come here in the first place? Did you know Whitaker?"

"Nope, never saw him before the boat. George here found a French rolled cigar stub in an ashtray in Slavinsky's apartment and remembered Whitaker smoked them. Then Slavinsky's landlady mentioned a fellow had been there last week that matched Whitaker's description, and I put two and two together. A little money, and the guy at the dock told me Whitaker and his aunt were spending the night here, so here we are."

"Good observation on your part, George, about the cigars," I admitted.

George grinned. "Thanks, Mr. B. I took the butt with me. Got it right here with me in my pocket—want to see it?"

"Thanks, maybe later. As for you, Ballentine, I'm impressed you can add two and two."

"I don't appreciate your insults, Barrington. I'm an educated man, finished tenth grade. So, how did you end up here? Obviously you found something out about Whitaker, too, or you wouldn't be here neither."

"Either."

"What?"

"Forget it, they probably covered that in the eleventh grade. Do you know where Whitaker's aunt is?"

"She ain't here, Detective. Maybe she shot him," George answered.

I looked at Ballentine and George grimly. "Maybe she did, and that's what I'm afraid of. There are too many questions and no answers."

"Can we put our arms down now? You already took our guns."

"And my brass knuckles and my switchblade," George added, sounding like a boy who has had his favorite toys taken away.

"All right, boys, but no sudden moves."

"So, now what?"

"Now I think it's time you take a ride downtown."

"On what charges?"

"I already told you—destroying private property, trespassing, breaking and entering, oh, and suspicion of murder."

"Murder? Of Whitaker? Why would we kill him? We didn't even know him, and we already told you we didn't kill Gregor."

"Another good question without an answer yet."

"Well, I've got an answer for you. We didn't do it and you know it. Go ahead and arrest us, Detective. I'll be out tomorrow at the latest. I've got connections. I'm a legitimate businessman these days. I own property, businesses, I'm a taxpayer, check my record."

"Don't think I won't, Ballentine. Is there a phone in this place?" I asked, ignoring him.

"Not that we could see, Mr. Benson," George said.

"Keyes, go to the office and call for a black-and-white on Mr. Nelson's phone."

"Yes, sir."

"Tell them to call the morgue, too. Better get Whitaker on ice. Have them contact Riker and let him know we've got Ballentine. Ask him to head over to the train station to look for Mrs. Woodfork. He knows what she looks like, and if I had to guess, I'd say she's headed out of town."

"Yes, sir."

"Get a black-and-white over to the bus depot, just in case, and put out an all-points bulletin. She should be considered armed and dangerous."

"That little old lady?" George asked, incredulous.

"Yes, George. You should know by now not to cross little old ladies. Get going, Keyes."

"Right away." He stepped out of the room and went quickly down the walk toward the office.

I backed away from George and Ballentine, keeping my gun on them while we waited for Keyes to return.

"So you think Slavinsky still had the money, eh, Ballentine?" I asked, making conversation.

"Yeah, and I want it back. It's legally mine, you know."

"That would be for the courts to decide, if the money can be found."

"He hid it somewhere, the bastard. He set me up, took advantage of our history together and my good nature."

I laughed. "I didn't know you had a good nature."

"It ain't funny, Detective. We were pals back then. We grew up together, worked together. I just happened to turn out more successful than he did, and I think he resented me for it."

"So when he got out of prison this last time, he concocted a scheme to sell you on a fake club he was planning on opening, and got you to loan him 25 Gs."

"I wouldn't have done it for nobody else, but Gregor and I had history together. I didn't figure he'd stab me in the back."

"It sounds like he stabbed you pretty well. I heard the building he said he was going to buy to use for the club wasn't even for sale."

"Yeah, the bastard. Then I found out he'd booked a ticket on that little boat headed for Michigan. Only I figured he was going to take my money and skip the country."

"So you decided to tag along."

"That's right. He kept playing it like the deal was still legit, that the building thing was all a misunderstanding, see? That he wasn't trying to cheat me, and part of me wanted to believe him. Otherwise, I would have shook him down before he even got on that dinghy and made him give me the money back, or made an example out of him."

"But you still had a little bit of trust and faith in you. I'm impressed."

"Gregor used up what little faith and trust I had, Detective."

"And then he went overboard."

"I never saw that coming, believe me. I didn't think he had it in him to commit suicide."

"And you don't know where the money is."

"No, but I can't see as how he spent it. Do you know where it is?" Ballentine asked.

"Not yet."

Just then Keyes, the two officers, and Mr. Nelson appeared at the door. "What about the boys from the morgue?" I asked.

"Right behind us, Detective."

"Morgue? What's happened?" Mr. Nelson asked, alarmed, as he glanced about the room that had been virtually torn apart.

"Mr. Nelson, I asked you to stay in your office," I admonished.

"I know, but when your officer friend here telephoned for more police, I thought I'd better see what's going on. Where are Mr. Whitaker and Mrs. Woodfork? And who's going to pay for all this damage?"

I looked at Keyes, standing next to him. Clearly he hadn't told him about Whitaker.

"I'd get in touch with your insurance company, Mr. Nelson. As for Mr. Whitaker, he's in the bathroom there, shot in the head. His aunt has disappeared."

Mr. Nelson looked from me to the bathroom door, to Ballentine and George, and back to me again. His face turned white, and I thought he might faint.

"Shot in the head? Here? In my motel? Oh, dear. You mean he's dead?"

"Not too many people survive bullets to the brain. It's not a pretty sight."

"Oh dear, oh dear, oh dear." He chewed vigorously on his toothpick, grinding it to splinters. "This won't be in the papers, will it? That's not good publicity. Business is tough enough as it is."

"We'll try to keep it quiet, but there's only so much we can do. The reporters have ways of sniffing out stuff like this. I'm frankly surprised they're not here already."

Mr. Nelson glanced about nervously, as if he expected reporters to pop out of the closet at any moment with camera flashbulbs exploding all over the place.

"Keyes, take Mr. Nelson back to his office and get him some water."

"Yes, sir." Keyes took Mr. Nelson's arm. "Let's go, sir. It will be all right."

The two of them walked out slowly, Mr. Nelson still looking like he'd faint and still shaking his head and saying, "Oh dear, oh dear, oh dear. I've never had any trouble here before. Oh dear, oh dear."

When they had gone, I nodded to the two officers from the black-and-white. "Take Mr. Ballentine to the squad car, boys. Then come back for George."

"Yes, sir." The tall one put the cuffs on Ballentine and George. "Let's go."

"Come on, George. We won't be locked up long," Ballentine said.

"George stays with me for a few minutes, Ballentine."

"What for?"

"None of your damned business."

"By the way, Detective, Slavinsky gave you his sister's contact information, didn't he?"

"That's right, why?"

"I'd like to send my condolences. Where in California did he say she's living?"

"Figure it out for yourself, Ballentine. For the record, I'm going to contact the state patrol in California and have them send a detective over to Slavinsky's sister's place."

"What for?"

"Because you threatened to harm her if Slavinsky didn't write that suicide note." I threw Keyes's theory at him, figuring it was worth a shot.

He looked at me blankly. "What are you talking about, Detective?"

"You used the threat to force him to write that note, didn't you? You think Slavinsky may have sent the money to her."

"I have no idea what you're on about. I never did no such thing. But now that you mention it, I wouldn't rule out the idea of him sending her the money."

"Exactly. So I'm not ruling it out, either, but I don't think he did."

"Why is that, Detective?"

"Because he wouldn't have mentioned her to me, and he certainly wouldn't have given me her contact information if she was implicated at all, even innocently."

"Maybe. Maybe not. Slavinsky's not all that smart."

"Unlike you, Ballentine. If you did force him to write that suicide note under the threat of harm to his family, I will find out. Get him the hell out of here, boys."

When they hauled Ballentine out, I walked over close to George. "How did you get messed up in all this, anyway?"

"I don't know what you're talking about, Mr. B."

"Ballentine, murder, crime. You're not stupid, remember?"

He shrugged. "He didn't kill anyone, Mr. B. Neither did I."

"I believe you're innocent, George. Loyal, but innocent. You'd do just about anything to protect him, wouldn't you?"

"Just about. But I didn't kill Mr. Whitaker."

"Slavinsky?"

"He killed himself, remember? We didn't force him to write that note. Why would we do that? The boss was pretty hot about him killing himself 'cause he didn't get his money back. Slavinsky had been making payments but got behind, and the boss didn't like that. And that club he was supposed to open didn't even exist."

"So when Slavinsky said he was taking that boat trip to Michigan, you two figured you had better go along and make sure he didn't get lost."

"That's right. We sure didn't figure he'd bump himself off, we really didn't. He just didn't seem the type. But then, the boss isn't real sympathetic with guys who go sour on their debts or try to cross him, either. Slavinsky knew that."

"So Ballentine figured the money might be hidden somewhere, huh?"

"Worth a shot. Hard to believe even a dope like Slavinsky could blow through that much in only a few months' time."

"That would seem unlikely."

The second policeman appeared in the doorway. "All set, Detective?"

"Just a moment."

I walked closer to George and spoke so that only he could hear. "What if someone were to bail you out tonight, before Ballentine can get his buddies to get him out?"

"Huh?"

"It would give you a chance, George, a start."

"To do what, Mr. B?"

"Anything. To get away from here, from him."

George stared at me thoughtfully. "I wouldn't have no place to go. He's all I've got, Mr. Benson. I'd be lost without him."

"You'd find your way, George. You're a smart guy, remember?"

He nodded slowly.

I continued. "Someday Ballentine will be locked up so tight no amount of money or connections will be able to get him out, or something else may happen to him. What then?"

George shrugged, still staring at me.

"Promise me you'll think about it."

He cocked his head. "Why would you want to help me?"

"Because I think there's more to you than this, George. Because I think there's more to you than even you realize."

"You're a nice man, Mr. Benson, thanks. I guess I better go, though. Mr. Ballentine doesn't like to be kept waiting."

I sighed. "Yeah, sure, George." I turned and spoke to the officer. "All right, take him away. I confiscated their weapons, too. Be sure and catalog them," I said, handing him the two revolvers, brass knuckles, and knife. "Have the lab check the guns to see if they've been fired recently."

"Yes, sir."

After they left, Keyes and I looked at each other, then at the mess scattered about the room.

"So they didn't find what they were looking for here either," Keyes stated.

"Apparently not."

"What would Slavinsky have done with all that cash, sir?"

"Maybe he did spend it. Maybe he gambled it or made a bad investment."

"Maybe, but it doesn't seem likely, does it?"

"No, it doesn't. And who killed Whitaker?"

Alan looked at me with those beautiful blue eyes of his. "Maybe the aunt shot him, or I guess maybe Miss Springer dressed as the aunt. She must have been gone when Ballentine and George arrived, and they said Whitaker was already dead."

"Supposedly. The coroner will be able to tell us more accurately how long he's been dead. We know Miss Springer was desperate for money. What was it Miss Lamb said? A girl's got to do what a girl's got to do."

"So she and Whitaker killed Slavinksy, and then she killed Whitaker. Wowzer."

"Wowzer indeed, Keyes."

We glanced about the room. "Ballentine and George certainly make a mess where ever they go, don't they, sir?"

"Yeah, they even ripped open the mattresses on the beds, the idiots."

Mr. Nelson reappeared at the door, still looking quite ill. "Excuse me, gentlemen, but the police station just called. An Officer Riker has located Mrs. Woodfork at the train depot, and he wanted to let you know. He said he is standing by."

"Roger that, thanks, Mr. Nelson. Let's go, Keyes. Looks like the coroner's team has just arrived."

After the briefest of discussions, we left them to do their job taking photographs and fingerprints, removing the body, and securing the room.

CHAPTER NINETEEN

The train depot's on the east end of Wisconsin, so we should be able to get there in about fifteen minutes." The two of us sprinted to my car and sped away, me behind the wheel and Keyes in the passenger seat.

As we drove quickly toward the station, Keyes looked over at me. "So how did you know Mrs. Woodfork was really Miss Springer? And when did you know?"

"I didn't know for certain. I still don't, but I had my suspicions, even on board. Riker found women's fashion magazines in Woodfork's and Whitaker's cabin, which seemed odd to me."

"Oh?"

"Yes. It seemed odd that an old lady, especially one who dressed as old-fashioned as Mrs. Woodfork did, would keep up on the latest styles. A woman like Trudy, however, would. She obviously brought them along to read in the privacy of their cabin. And Mrs. Woodfork wore her black gloves constantly, even at dinner. If there's one thing my Aunt Verbina taught me, it's that a lady would never eat wearing gloves, even in mourning."

"Why do you think she wore the gloves all the time?"

"Because even an expert makeup man like Baines would

have trouble making a thirty-year-old woman's hands look like those of a seventy- or eighty-year-old."

"Gee, I never would have picked up on that, Heath."

"Oh, I don't know. You're sharper than you give yourself credit for, Alan."

"Thanks. I appreciate that, but I have a lot to learn from you yet."

I looked at him and smiled. "And I you. It was also odd that she wore the hat, veil, and dark glasses all the time, even indoors. At first I thought it was due to a medical condition—light sensitivity or something like that, but it was more to disguise the youthful Miss Springer."

He turned away for a bit, gazing out the window at the scenery whizzing by, pondering, and then he looked back to me. "So Miss Springer and Baines killed Slavinsky and she killed Baines and took the money. Was she really that desperate?"

"That's a good question I think I know the answer to, but I'm not certain quite yet. We're almost to the station. Riker said she's on a bench on the platform, waiting for the night train to upper Michigan and on to Canada. I'm parking in front. I want you to stay with the car."

"What for?"

"You can keep people outside and out of the way. Besides, this could get dangerous."

"If it gets dangerous in there, you need me with you. You're not the best shot, as I recall."

"I'll manage, and Riker's in there. Please stay out here and keep folks out of harm's way."

"All right, sir, but keep yourself out of harm's way first."

I smiled. "I intend to do my best. I have a wedding to attend in sixty or seventy years."

I brought my Buick to a halt in a No Parking zone near

the front door, and I turned off the engine. I entered the main hall of the beautiful Romanesque building as the clock in the tower struck eight. Riker, still looking handsome in his police uniform, was waiting for me. We wasted no time on pleasantries.

"Is she still out there?"

"Yes, sir. What's happened? Where is her nephew?"

"Whitaker's dead. I'll fill you in on the rest later. Have your gun ready and be on guard. Let's go."

We walked swiftly through the crowded terminal to the platform door where, much to my dismay, a full complement of passengers waited on the next train. Mrs. Woodfork was easy enough to spot, though. She was sitting alone on a bench, still dressed exactly the same, with the carpetbag at her feet.

The angle of the bench made it impossible to approach her stealthily, so I opted for the straightforward approach. "Stay behind me, Riker. I'm going to make contact. She may try to make a run for it or get violent. I don't want any innocent bystanders getting hurt."

"That little old lady?"

"Unless I am seriously mistaken, that is no old lady."

"Yes, sir. I think I understand. I'm a crack shot, if need be."

"Good." I walked boldly up to where she sat. She looked at me through those dark glasses and the veil with what I assumed was a startled expression as her mouth dropped open. Otherwise, it was impossible to tell.

"Good evening, Mrs. Woodfork. Remember me? Detective Barrington from the boat?"

She nodded.

"And that's Officer Riker, also from the boat." I gestured over my shoulder. "Do you mind if I ask you some questions?"

She turned her head, clearly looking for a means of escape

before looking back to me. "All right. My voice is a little better today, though still hoarse. Ask what you will," she said.

"I thought you and your nephew were going to take the train tomorrow."

"I decided not to wait. My nephew will join me tomorrow."

"Can't get away fast enough, eh? You said before that you were asleep all night last night on the boat, is that correct?"

"Yes, that's right. I'd taken a pill and slept all night until that nasty incident with that man going overboard, anyway."

"And you weren't familiar with Gregor Slavinsky prior to yesterday."

"Not at all, though he seemed pleasant enough, I suppose. I suspect what happened to him was just fate."

"Fate?"

"His time. Have you ever noticed how someone can fall off a five-story building and get up and walk away with barely a scratch, but someone else can fall off a curb, hit their head, and die? It's all preordained, I think. Or if not luck, call it fate. He was predestined to take his own life. What was it you said earlier? Life is kismet, a turn of the roulette wheel, a roll of the dice."

"A deal of the cards," I finished for her. "Yes, that's right. Only I never said that to you, Mrs. Woodfork. I said it to Gregor Slavinsky before you were even aboard."

From behind me I heard the train approaching. Bad timing, certainly. The platform would soon be teeming with even more people getting off and hurrying to board.

"Mr. Slavinsky must have mentioned your comment to me," she said quietly, and I strained to hear over the sounds of the platform and the oncoming train.

I shook my head. "Unlikely, because you are Mr. Slavinsky, aren't you? And Ballentine's money is in that carpetbag at your feet, and right now you're under arrest for fraud and two counts of suspicion of murder."

The train screeched to a halt beside us, and I momentarily turned my head toward it, but it was just enough time. From a pocket in the dress, Slavinsky pulled a small revolver and aimed it right at me. I instinctively reached for mine, but someone pushed me before I could draw it. A shot rang out, then another.

I spun around, recovering from the shove, and drew my own gun, holding it now on Slavinsky, who had toppled off the bench and fallen to the ground, his wig now askew. Several women on the platform screamed, and a conductor came running up to me. Blood was pouring from Slavinsky's chest. His gun had slid off the platform and beneath the train.

I looked at the conductor. "Get an ambulance and see if there's a doctor somewhere near—make an announcement. I'm Detective Barrington with the Milwaukee Police."

"Yes, sir." The conductor turned and made his way through the crowd that had formed around us. Everyone seemed to be talking at once, asking questions, pushing in to see what had happened.

"Riker!" I shouted. "Get these people away and call for backup." I kept my gun and my eyes on Slavinsky, his chest heaving, blood spurting out.

Riker did not respond.

"Riker!"

"I think the officer's been shot as well, sir," said a young boy who had been selling evening newspapers.

I scanned the crowd and then the ground, where indeed Riker was lying a short distance behind me, facedown in a pool of blood.

"You!" I shouted at the young boy. "Run outside and

tell the policeman who's standing out there. Tell him I need backup, and tell him to get in here right away."

The boy hurried away, leaving his newspaper sack behind.

The loudspeaker overhead crackled to life, and I heard a man's voice calling for a doctor to the platform.

An older man pushed through the crowd, carrying a dark satchel. "I'm a doctor. What's happened here?"

"These two men have been shot, Doctor. Tend to the officer first."

"But the lady."

"That's no lady. It's a man in disguise, a murderer. There's no time to waste with explanations."

The doctor stepped behind me and knelt down by Riker, turning him gently over. As I felt my stomach heave, I thought momentarily that I might be sick. I couldn't bear to look.

The doctor applied a bandage to Riker's head, then stood up and approached me, his demeanor calm and professional. "He'll be all right, but he's a lucky one. The bullet grazed his temple and the fall must have knocked him unconscious. I'll have to do a more thorough exam, of course, and he most likely has a concussion, but he's in no immediate danger. I need to check on that other fellow right away, though. He looks in bad shape."

I nodded, feeling relief pour through me. "Go ahead."

Soon Keyes and two other officers were pushing through the crowd, yelling at everyone to stand back. "Heath! I'm so glad you're all right. The boy said someone was shot." I could see the relief in his eyes.

"Looks like Slavinsky and Riker shot each other. Riker shoved me out of the way."

"Will they be all right?"

"Sounds like Riker will be, but it's too soon to tell on

Slavinsky. Where did those two come from?" I gestured toward the policemen now dispersing the crowd.

"They came by out front, lucky thing, too."

"It looks like the guys from the ambulance are here now." Two young men in white jackets and pants elbowed their way to us, carrying a stretcher. "Better get Slavinsky out of here and to the hospital. Send another for Officer Riker, please. Have one of those officers accompany Slavinsky in the ambulance. I don't think he's a threat in the condition he's in, but he is under arrest, and I want a guard on him at all times."

"Understood, sir."

The two men got Slavinsky on the stretcher and carried him out, the wound in his chest bandaged as best as the doctor could manage under the circumstances, and the police officer applying pressure to the wound per one of the drivers' instructions. Four more officers arrived shortly after, and I was thankful for the assist, as a couple of reporters had shown up and were trying to get photographs of Riker still lying on the platform. The bandage on Riker's temple was now soaked with blood, and the doctor was kneeling by him again, checking his vital signs. I knelt on the other side of him while Keyes stood by.

"How's he doing, Doc?"

"He's stable. The bleeding seems to have stopped. He's a very lucky man. If that bullet had been half an inch to the left, he may have been killed."

I gazed down at the beautiful man, his hair matted with blood, as his eyes fluttered open.

"Hey, you," I said softly, tears in my eyes.

"Heath, you okay?"

I laughed lightly, embarrassed by my emotions. "I'm fine, thanks to you. You're going to be okay, too—just a graze, but they're going to take you to the hospital soon to make sure everything's good."

"Glad to hear it. I don't feel so good, and I probably look worse."

"You look fine, Officer. We'll call your wife and have her meet you at the hospital."

"Yeah, she'll be worried."

"You had me worried, too, Riker. But that was good shooting on your part. You took Slavinsky down. He's already on his way to the hospital, in far worse shape than you."

"All instinct, Heath. I just reacted."

"Don't try to talk too much right now," the doctor said. "You'll need to stay awake until we can fully examine you, though, as much as you may want to sleep."

"I appreciate your assistance, Doc. I hope you didn't miss your train," I said.

"I did, but there will be other trains. I'll leave him in the care of the doctors at the hospital once the second ambulance arrives."

"I think they're here now, Heath," Keyes said.

Two more men in white approached with another stretcher.

"Looks like your ride is here, Riker."

"Is that your friend?" Riker whispered as I bent to hear him.

I looked up at Keyes, standing by my side, his hand on my shoulder. "Yes, my good friend."

"The someone waiting for you back home?"

I nodded.

"He's a lucky guy."

"So am I, Riker, so am I. And so are you."

I stood and let the ambulance men get him carefully onto the stretcher.

"See you around, Heath. Don't take any wooden nickels."

"I suspect you'll make detective before you know it, Riker." I smiled at him and he did his best to smile back.

"Thanks. Maybe we can work on another case together someday."

"You never know."

I stood with Keyes as we watched them carry him back into the terminal and out to the ambulance.

As they were going out, Fletch and his team were coming in, and I was glad to see them. Fletch walked up to me, relief on his face that I was all right.

"Looks like you dodged a bullet, Detective."

"Funny, Fletch, but yeah, thanks to Riker. Who called you down here?"

"The second group of officers called in the shooting, along with some hysterical lady from a pay phone inside the depot. Dispatch sent me and the boys out to see if assistance was needed."

"It definitely is, Fletch. By the way, this is Officer Keyes."

Fletch looked him up and down. "Pretty much what I expected. Nice to meet you."

Alan shook his hand but looked perplexed.

"I'll explain it to you later, Keyes. Fletch, I believe the suspect's gun went onto the tracks. Be careful handling it. I want it dusted for prints so there's no doubt. And see if you can figure out where the bullet that grazed Riker went. We may need that for evidence, too."

"Sure thing, Heath. You look like hell."

"Thanks."

Fletch turned and walked up the platform, barking orders to his assistant, and I turned wearily to Alan.

"I guess that's it, then, Heath."

I nodded slowly. "Yes, this time I think it's truly over. I'll have to edit my report, fill the chief in, file paperwork, and check on Riker."

"You've barely slept, and we haven't eaten since noon."

"I know. I think I'll take tomorrow off. In the meantime, let's go get a bite to eat and a cup of coffee. It will keep me awake. How about Lucky Liu's? It's just up the street."

"I thought they closed," Alan said.

"They did for a while. The war was hard on them, definitely not lucky. People had difficulty discerning between the Chinese and the Japanese. Anyone who looked Oriental was treated as an enemy by some ignorant people, and sadly there are a lot of ignorant people in the world. In actuality, over thirteen thousand Chinese served in all branches of the U.S. Army during the war, and many lost their lives."

"Then let's go to Lucky Liu's."

"You got it, Keyes, let's go!"

CHAPTER TWENTY

We took a ride to Lucky Liu's on west Wisconsin Avenue and parked ourselves in a booth. As we sipped our hot black coffee and waited for our eggrolls, Keyes looked over at me.

"What? Do I look that bad? Do I really look like hell?"

"Not at all, Heath. I was just thinking, though, that you did it again. You solved another case."

"We solved it, Alan."

"Thanks, but you knew Slavinsky wasn't murdered and didn't commit suicide."

"And yet in a way he did, Keyes."

"What do you mean?"

"Gregor Slavinsky killed off Gregor Slavinsky, or at least he tried to."

"Sure, I guess so. He was clever, but not as clever as you. You figured it all out."

"Again with your help, Alan. And Riker's. I just knew something didn't seem right."

"But what tipped you off?"

I took another sip of coffee before answering. "Lots of little things, actually. Gregor took the money from Ballentine with no intention of repaying it. He got in touch with Baines, knowing he was a makeup artist, and probably offered him a certain amount of cash for his part in all this. Gregor asked him to find an actress similar in physique and appearance to Slavinsky, who would be willing to play the part of Mrs. Woodfork—preferably someone who wouldn't be missed if she disappeared. Trudy Springer was the perfect candidate because she had no family and, presumably, no friends except Miss Lamb. Slavinsky, Baines, and Miss Springer probably met for coffee, then went back to Gregor's place for a trial fitting and makeup test, which is when Slavinsky's landlady spotted them."

"Of course. The big bag had the makeup and wig in it."

"Yes. The dress, gloves, and the rest of the getup probably came later. The idea of her being in mourning was clever—a good excuse to dress her in a veil and dark hat. Then there was that headshot of Mrs. Woodfork that Riker found in their cabin. Remember Mrs. Price mentioned Baines had a camera with him. He took Trudy's photograph once she was all made up, knowing he would need that as reference when he made Slavinsky up. The well-placed beauty mark, the pale white skin, the dark glasses, the strong violet perfume—all things they knew people would identify Mrs. Woodfork with."

"Wowzer. They'd identify those things with her, making it easier for Slavinksy to take over the role."

"Yes, exactly. And the cameo choker conveniently hid Slavinsky's Adam's apple. I also thought the bottle of whiskey in Gregor's cabin was strange, as he drank martinis. Whitaker was the one who liked whiskey, but of course he didn't want to risk Trudy finding his bottle and getting smashed, so he kept it in Gregor's cabin and used the connecting door to move back and forth without being seen."

"Do you think Trudy knew Slavinsky was going to dress as her, to take over the part?"

"Not likely. I'm sure they both told her all she needed to do was play the role of sickly old Mrs. Woodfork and pretend she'd never met Slavinsky."

"Jeepers. So she agreed to play the part never knowing it would be her final role."

"Sadly, yes."

"Any other clues?"

"Lots, in retrospect. I didn't put them all together at first. There was Slavinsky's book on the Great Lakes, for example."

"Why the book?"

"Riker said he had been charting the boat's course in it, but I suspect he wanted to chart our course because he was planning to throw the body overboard at one of the deepest points in the lake. His sudden beard and mustache made me suspicious, too."

"Why?" Alan asked, sipping his coffee.

"He had apparently never had facial hair before. You had mentioned that maybe he was trying to disguise himself, which made me think that perhaps he was trying to look as different from Mrs. Woodfork as he possibly could, so that when he assumed the role, it wouldn't be as noticeable."

"He really thought it out, didn't he?"

"Yes, he did. I believe he or probably Baines slipped Trudy the phenobarbital sometime during the night, causing her to sleep deeply. They most likely strangled or smothered her, dressed her in Slavinsky's clothing, added some weights, and threw her overboard. Then, with Slavinsky newly shaved, they dressed him in Mrs. Woodfork's costume and wig and made him up to look like her, using the photo as reference. I was suspicious that Mrs. Woodfork always wore a veil and hat and thick makeup, and she rarely spoke except in hoarse whispers. They didn't want anyone getting a really good look at her so no one would notice when Slavinsky took her place."

"Amazing and cold."

"Very cold. You almost had it figured out when you said perhaps Miss Springer was pretending to be Slavinsky and Slavinsky was Mrs. Woodfork."

"Thanks. But you're the one who put it all together, Heath."

"I guess so. I feel sorry for Trudy. The poor girl could never get a break. Here she thought she had an easy role and easy money, and she ends up dead. Baines cold-bloodedly selected Trudy because she was close in height, weight, and appearance to Slavinsky, and because she had acting experience and could play the role of Mrs. Woodfork convincingly. All the while he knew she wouldn't make it off the boat alive and wouldn't be missed much by anyone."

"It is pretty sad, Heath. Even her roommate wouldn't have missed her for several weeks. And when she never returned, well, I doubt anyone would much care or investigate if an alcoholic actress and paid escort turned up missing."

"Yes, very sad. When the boat docked back in Milwaukee, Baines and Slavinsky went to the motel, where they probably planned to lay low until the next day and then split the money and go their separate ways—Slavinsky off to Canada, where he could get lost, and Baines back to his makeup job."

"So how did Baines end up dead?"

I shrugged. "Hard to say for sure what happened. I suspect Slavinsky got greedy and wanted Baines out of the way. Besides, Baines was the only one that knew Slavinsky was still alive. They went back to the motel to sort things out, Slavinsky took out his gun and shot him dead."

"What about the carpetbag?"

"That made me wonder, too. Slavinsky obviously took the cash on board in his own suitcase. Of course he didn't want to keep it on his person or in his cabin because he feared

Ballentine would find it. So he gave it to Baines, who kept it in the carpetbag. After they murdered Trudy, Slavinsky took possession of the bag and was planning on slipping away to Canada with it, only as Mrs. Woodfork."

"But he wasn't expecting Ballentine and George to be on board."

"Oh, I think he was *counting* on Ballentine and George to be there."

"Huh?"

"He booked his passage under his own name and let it be known he was going away. He wanted Ballentine and George to come along, and he wanted them to think he was planning on slipping out of the country."

"Why would he want that? Why not just slip away?"

"Because if he did that, Ballentine and George would look for him and he'd be hiding forever. But if they thought he was dead, he could be a free man with twenty-five grand. He figured he'd take over the role of Mrs. Woodfork, and he and Baines would get off in Michigan and never look back. They'd get into the car Slavinsky had arranged and drive over the border, where Slavinsky would ditch the Woodfork costume. He probably planned on killing Baines somewhere along the way."

"But the boat had to return to Milwaukee."

"Yes, much to Slavinsky's chagrin, I'm sure. He hadn't counted on me being on deck when the body went overboard, either, so he probably figured him being missing wouldn't be discovered until morning, when they were almost to Michigan or even already docked, and there was no turning back."

"Lucky thing you were on deck."

"Not so lucky for him. Mr. Whitaker and Mrs. Woodfork were late in getting to the lounge after the body went overboard. Riker and I had been in the wheelhouse for some time, then

Riker went down, and when I went in the lounge everyone was there except the two of them. They eventually showed up, fully dressed."

"Curious."

"Yes. In actuality, Baines had already been dressed, of course, but they needed time to make Slavinsky up as Mrs. Woodfork. If I hadn't been on deck, they would have had the rest of the night to prepare, so I definitely caused a problem."

I finished my coffee, turning down a refill as the waitress brought our eggrolls and rice. We ate quickly, both of us hungrier than we'd realized. When we were finished, Keyes looked over at me. "You didn't open your fortune cookie."

"Neither did you," I countered.

"All right. Mine says, 'Enjoy the good luck a companion brings you.'"

"Nice. Mine says, 'A chance meeting opens new doors to success and friendship.'"

"Well. there you have it, Heath."

"Yes, lots of chance meetings, lots of new doors, lots of companionship."

"All good stuff, Heath. I suppose we'd better head to the station now, huh? The chief will be looking for you."

"I'm sure. And then I want to go to the hospital to check on Riker. You don't have to come me with if you don't want to. It's late."

"I do want to."

"Okay."

"Riker's a handsome man," Keyes stated.

"Some would think so."

"Do you think so?"

I nodded. "I do. He's a good policeman, too. In many ways, he's a lot like you. But there's one important difference, Keyes."

"What's that?"

"He's not you."

Keyes smiled at me, his eyes sparkling. "I'm glad to hear that, Detective."

"You ready?" I asked.

"To go?"

"Yes, and for whatever may come."

"As long as you're beside me, I'll be ready."

"Same here. Then let's go."

I paid the bill, and we left the restaurant without another word, both of us knowing nothing else needed to be said.

About the Author

David S. Pederson was born in Leadville, Colorado, where his father was a miner. Soon after, the family relocated to Wisconsin, where David grew up, attending high school and university, majoring in business and creative writing. Landing a job in retail, he found himself relocating to New York, Massachusetts, and eventually back to Wisconsin, where he currently lives with his husband and works in the furniture and decorating business.

He has written many short stories and poetry and is passionate about mysteries, old movies, and crime novels. When not reading, writing, or working in the furniture business, David also enjoys working out and studying classic ocean liners, floor plans, and historic homes.

David can be contacted at davidspederson@gmail.com or dspederson@sbcglobal.net.

Visit his website at http://www.davidspederson.com.

Books Available From Bold Strokes Books

Death Goes Overboard by David S. Pederson. Heath Barrington and Alan Keyes are two sides of a steamy love triangle as they encounter gangsters, con men, murder, and more aboard an old lake steamer. (978-1-62639-907-5)

A Careful Heart by Ralph Josiah Bardsley. Be careful what you wish for...love changes everything. (978-1-62639-887-0)

Worms of Sin by Lyle Blake Smythers. A haunted mental asylum turned drug treatment facility exposes supernatural detective Finn M'Coul to an outbreak of murderous insanity, a strange parasite, and ghosts that seek sex with the living. (978-1-62639-823-8)

Tartarus by Eric Andrews-Katz. When Echidna, Mother of all Monsters, escapes from Tartarus and into the modern world, only an Olympian has the power to oppose her. (978-1-62639-746-0)

Rank by Richard Compson Sater. Rank means nothing to the heart, but the Air Force isn't as impartial. Every airman learns that rank has its privileges. What about love? (978-1-62639-845-0)

The Grim Reaper's Calling Card by Donald Webb. When Katsuro Tanaka begins investigating the disappearance of a young nurse, he discovers more missing persons, and they all have one thing in common: The Grim Reaper Tarot Card. (978-1-62639-748-4)

Smoldering Desires by C.E. Knipes. Evan McGarrity has found the man of his dreams in Sebastian Tantalos. When an old boyfriend from Sebastian's past enters the picture, Evan must fight for the man he loves. (978-1-62639-714-9)

Tallulah Bankhead Slept Here by Sam Lollar. A coming of age/coming out story, set in El Paso of 1967, that tells of Aaron's adventures with movie stars, cool cars, and topless bars. (978-1-62639-710-1)

Death Came Calling by Donald Webb. When private investigator Katsuro Tanaka is hired to look into the death of a high-profile lawyer, he becomes embroiled in a case of murder and mayhem. (978-1-60282-979-4)

The City of Seven Gods by Andrew J. Peters. In an ancient city of aerie temples, a young priest and a barbarian mercenary struggle to refashion their lives after their worlds are torn apart by betrayal. (978-1-62639-775-0)

Lysistrata Cove by Dena Hankins. Jack and Eve navigate the maelstrom of their darkest desires and find love by transgressing gender, dominance, submission, and the law on the crystal blue Caribbean Sea. (978-1-62639-821-4)

Garden District Gothic by Greg Herren. Scotty Bradley has to solve a notorious thirty-year-old unsolved murder that has terrible repercussions in the present. (978-1-62639-667-8)

The Man on Top of the World by Vanessa Clark. Jonathan Maxwell falling in love with Izzy Rich, the world's hottest glam rock superstar, is not only unpredictable but complicated when a bold teenage fan-girl changes everything. (978-1-62639-699-9)

The Orchard of Flesh by Christian Baines. With two hotheaded men under his roof including his werewolf lover, a vampire tries to solve an increasingly lethal mystery while keeping Sydney's supernatural factions from the brink of war. (978-1-62639-649-4)

Funny Bone by Daniel W. Kelly. Sometimes sex feels so good you just gotta giggle! (978-1-62639-683-8)

The Thassos Confabulation by Sam Sommer. With the inheritance of a great deal of money, David and Chris also inherit a nondescript brown paper parcel and a strange and perplexing letter that sends David on a quest to understand its meaning. (978-1-62639-665-4)

The Photographer's Truth by Ralph Josiah Bardsley. Silicon Valley tech geek Ian Baines gets more than he bargained for on an unexpected journey of self-discovery through the lustrous nightlife of Paris. (978-1-62639-637-1)

Crimson Souls by William Holden. A scorned shadow demon brings a centuries-old vendetta to a bloody end as he assembles the last of the descendants of Harvard's Secret Court. (978-1-62639-628-9)

$$\frac{\ddot{\smile}\ /3}{1\ \ 88}$$
191